the
AIRDANCER
of GLASS

This book is Catherine's first speculative fiction novel and draws on her experience of growing up in Queensland at a time when environmental issues were just beginning to be of great concern. Catherine Bateson now lives in the Latrobe Valley with her two children and is reminded daily of both the natural beauty of the world and our destruction of it.

Catherine Bateson

the AIRDANCER of GLASS

UQP

First published 2004 by University of Queensland Press
Box 6042, St Lucia, Queensland 4067 Australia

www.uqp.uq.edu.au

Typeset by University of Queensland Press
Printed in Australia by McPherson's Printing Group

Distributed in the USA and Canada by
International Specialized Books Services, Inc.,
5824 N.E. Hassalo Street, Portland, Oregon 97213—3640

This project has been assisted by
the Commonwealth Government through
the Australia Council, its arts fundind
and advisory body.

Cataloguing in Publication Data
National Library of Australia

Bateson, Catherine.
  The airdancer of glass.

  For young adults.
  I. Title.

A823.3

ISBN 0 7022 3393 5

*For Pauline who was there from the beginning,
for Andrew — with thanks for the rockets —
and, In Memoriam, Robert David Hill (1926—2003)*

Once upon a time, before the Final War and before the Contaminations, there were Super Markets and you could buy anything you needed. Everyone had a special job and got paid for it, even quite small children. It was the age of plenty and people were happy all the time. Then the Contaminations came, wave after wave, released by the enemies. When the Wars started the Fatters built Glass to keep themselves safe. They said everyone outside would die but we didn't. Tip didn't die because Tippers are tough. We have to be.

from *The Lessons of Amos from North Tip,*
Healer and Revolutionary

'C'm here.' The man beckoned the girl who watched him from the other side of the small fire.

'C'm on, Lulu, I won't hurt you.'

'No, Nemrick,' she said.

'A man gets lonely,' he said. 'Since Birdie died I've never. Well, hardly. Anyway, it's you I want, Lulu. C'm over here, baby. Warm me up. Let's both warm up.'

'No.' Lulianne wasn't even sure if Nemrick could hear her. She kept her distance, kept the fire between them, moving left when he moved right, sure-footed where he stumbled. She knew from recent experience that Nemrick could keep this up practically until the end of the bottle, then he'd suddenly fall, felled by the voddy, still groping for her until he passed out, cradling the bottle.

'I've been like a father to you,' Nemrick whined. 'I've done everything for you. You could do just this one thing for me.'

'No.' She kept circling warily. Sometimes the voddy gave

1

him a spurt of unexpected strength and agility before he collapsed. Or perhaps he pretended to be more drunk than he really was.

'It's just us,' he said. 'Just us in this bloody dump and you won't even give a man comfort.'

'It's not just us, there's Archer and Guz. We're all family, Nemrick. We're all circus.'

'Ha! Circus! Up and down the coast from Defence to Glass and back again. Unless we die like Birdie. Poor bloody Birdie. Poor dear Birdie. I miss her, Lulu, I miss Birdie so much.'

Nemrick collapsed then, on his knees, still holding the bottle. He looked up at the stars, and in the small flickers of firelight Lulianne could see tears rolling down his face.

'We all miss her,' she said, moving towards him in spite of herself. He was, after all, her teacher, almost a father, and she hated to see him crying even if they were drunk tears.

When she got close enough she put her hand out to touch his shoulder and just seconds too late saw his eyes gleam sharply beneath the tears. He grabbed her and pulled her down on top of him.

'Let go!' she shouted. 'Let go, you bastard.'

'Gottcha, pretty one,' he said. 'Got my Lulu.' He pushed her right back on to the ground beside him, grabbing both her wrists in one big, strong hand. The grip of his thumbs was cruel.

She twisted her head away from his mouth and he couldn't let go her wrists to make her meet his kisses. He could break her wrists if he wanted to, and he might, if he became angry enough so she stopped struggling and let herself go limp. An airdancer couldn't risk a broken wrist. An airdancer couldn't court injury. Look what had happened to Birdie. Anything was better than that.

'You'll hate yourself in the morning,' she said, talking loudly, trying to slow down her words so the fear in her voice was masked. 'You'll really be sorry, Nemrick. You don't want this. You know you don't want this. You're just hurting, we're all hurting over Birdie. You don't want me, you want Birdie. And you know Birdie would hate what you're doing.'

'I loved Birdie,' Nemrick said, anchoring her firmly on the ground with his own body. He took a swig of voddy. 'I loved Birdie and she loved me. She'd want anything I wanted.'

'If you force me, you're as bad as those soldiers. And they really killed Birdie.'

'No,' Nemrick said, 'they didn't even know her. We're family, Lulu. That's different. I love you. I loved Birdie too, but she's gone, flown away. So now I love you.'

'You don't love me, Nemrick,' Lulianne said firmly. 'You just miss Birdie and you're lonely and cold.'

'That's right,' Nemrick said. 'Oh, that's right, Lulu. Some nights the emptiness is too much. It eats into my bones. I've got nothing without her. Just this ache and this mangy, hungry life. I miss her so much.' Nemrick began to sob. His body went limp and his tears fell on Lulianne's face.

She wanted to hold him but was still afraid, so lay motionless, trapped as much by the man's grief as by his weight and strength. A stone jammed into the back of her thigh but she ignored it and concentrated on the stars she could see over Nemrick's shoulder. Only when his head fell to one side and the last moaning sob became a breathy snore did she begin to slide slowly and gently from underneath him.

Then she stretched and shook herself, loosening the tension from her muscles, gently massaging her most painful cramped limbs. She prodded the snoring man with her foot. He didn't budge. His mouth was open, half-pressed into the ground as though he were about to kiss the ashy, dry earth. He deserved to sleep like that. Later, when the voddy nightmares shook him out of sleep, he'd wake with a mouthful of dirt. Serve him right.

'I'm going. I'm leaving, Nemrick. I can't take this night after night. One time you're going to get home too early, not quite drunk enough but too drunk to care, too drunk to stop and then what will happen to me? I don't want to mate with you. I love you, poor old man, but not like that. Do you hear me?' He didn't hear her. She kicked him, hard enough to bruise, but he just groaned without waking.

Lulianne didn't have much to put in the light pack she carried. There were her airdancing ropes, her harness and her costume. From the kitchen tent she took a water bottle, plate and fork and filled a billy with hard biscuits and dried meat strips. Birdie's knife and her own papers she carried in a soft pouch around her waist, hidden under her clothes. For sentimental and practical reasons she took one of the soft old rag rugs Birdie had woven from costume scraps. They spread out the rugs sometimes for people to drop their offerings on.

She stopped to say goodbye to the camels they'd travelled with. Flatfoot, the young mare she'd ridden and walked beside felt like her own but belonged to Circus and had to be left behind. Adri, the brindle bitch was her own though, and she wouldn't leave without Adri. Her mother had bought the pup and Lulianne loved her.

'Come on, girl,' she said, untethering her, 'we're off. Say goodbye to your pack mates, it's you and me now.' She used

4

the dog's rope to tie her swag beneath the light camel-hide pack, bent to tie her shoes more tightly and, without looking back, walked away from Circus Despoir.

'Bloody Nemrick,' she thought, settling the weight of the pack more firmly on her shoulders. 'Stupid old man.' Why had Nemrick spoiled everything?

The others — Archer, Guz and Lizard — couldn't help. Birdie had held them all together. Without her everything fell apart. They were all drinking gut-rot, the four men, every night. The cash they'd earned in Defence and Death was squandered on voddy, dope and liquid morph. Well, Lulianne could understand that. She'd swallowed a bottle or two for comfort, after Birdie.

Birdie had been their hope, made the present bearable and the future something to look forward to. She loved the air stunts, the crowd's applause and even the endless travelling. Birdie had loved life, that was her secret.

In the distance, Glass caught the starry night's light and reflected it back. All that was between Lulianne and the city were the mounds of Outside. Still, it was deceptive. Hours of walking lay ahead of her and she'd need to find somewhere to sleep, her feet were already hurting.

Scrub was better than mounds, the girl decided. She preferred to sleep in the scrub rather than the tip mounds.

'Don't like the smell of the mounds, do we, Adri?' she said to the great dog, more to hear the sound of her own voice than anything else. She shivered. She'd never been on her own before. Camping out had always meant the bustle of activity around her, setting up the little tents, tethering and settling the animals, and then later a shared meal and the idle talk around the fire.

Lulianne huddled down in her swag. The night seemed very big and each sound was amplified by the unending sky. Adri pawed the ground next to her.

'Come on Adri, you can sleep here for the night. We'll keep each other warm.'

Adri scrambled into the swag. Her fur was rough but warm and the dog smell familiar and safe. Outside smelled of rust and decayed lives even though the Contaminations were nearly a hundred years ago. The closer to Tip, outside Glass, the worse it would smell. She was grateful Adri was with her. Maybe Birdie was right, maybe there was always something to be thankful for while you could still draw breath.

'Good night, Adri,' Lulianne whispered. 'Goodnight, Birdie.' And resting her hand lightly on Birdie's knife as she had done every night since the older woman's death, Lulianne waited for sleep.

She reached North Tip late the following morning. As soon as Tip was visible, Lulianne changed into her circus costume, looping her dreads with ribbons and small bells, swapping her rough hide shoes for softer ones made out of brightly dyed feral skins. The blazing colours and the sheer impracticality of her flared skirt and tight bodice set her aside from the Tippers, whose clothes were stained grey, black and rust, just as the Tip was.

As soon as she came into North, children swarmed around her, reaching out to touch her clothes and hair. They pulled at her felt skirt, tugged at the bells in her hair. She wanted to swat them away. Usually she swayed in on the back of Flatfoot, flanked by the tumblers, Guz and Archer, with Nemrick holding Lizard above his head, the strong man with the bionic arm. Then the children kept a respectful distance and

6

if they didn't, well, Nemrick would roar at them and shake Lizard as though he were a weapon. That made the kids scatter back! By herself, she had to take a deep breath, hold her head up and walk high and proud, creating a space between herself and the curious children by her sheer presence.

'Come and see the airdancer,' she called out, as though the children weren't right in front of her. 'See her amazing flight through the air. Stick around, kids, and watch me fly.' Her voice sounded thin to her ears, but the children fell back and gave her more room. They followed her to the old Security Tower, where she planned on performing.

Birdie and Lulianne had a routine which was pure air-dancing. They worked together, and alone, harnessed and unharnessed, to show how gravity can be momentarily defeated by sheer strength, training and will. The flight from one to the other, the strictly choreographed rope-diving, the slow mid-air spins and somersaults, the human top, all were done in a dance that soared above the gaping crowd as though the dancers themselves had forgotten its existence. Birdie was only interested in flight. What we give them, she often said, is an illusion. Seeing us, they gain freedom.

Lulianne tested her rig, the ropes and harness which would transform the grim tower into her stage. She spread the faded orange rug, removed her fur shoes and told Adri to guard the takings as though totally unaware of the crowd that had formed at a more respectful distance now, the adults hushing children and dragging them back. When she was sure everything was in place, Lulianne turned to the crowd and acknowledged them with a small, proud bow.

'Today I bring you the airdancer Lulianne, most lately from Circus Despoir. Hold your breath, ladies and gentlemen, girls and boys, you are about to see the performance of a lifetime.' She bowed again and began to climb the metal struts inside the base of the tower right up until it narrowed into a space small enough to straddle.

Through the thin criss-crossed metal bars Lulianne could see over Glass right into the rooftop garden areas, the lush green shimmering through the glass. She stood spread-eagled here, both enjoying the view and giving the audience time to appreciate just how high up she was. The city of cubes made a fine view, a jigsaw of transparent and dark glass, some of which reflected the sky in enticing pools of cool blue and cloud. They looked as though you could dive into, or through, them.

Lulianne checked her harness and spread out her arms. Now that Birdie was dead, she was the only airdancer who still did this stunt — free-falling for about twenty metres — before actually starting the air dance. It was, Birdie insisted, one of the finest moments: the second of flight, then the downward rush, only just controlled by the harness ropes.

At fifteen metres Lulianne halted her fall, pulling hard on the harness. She swung gently from side to side and, working quickly, fixed the custom-made rigging to the metal struts of the tower. Once it was in place, she began to enjoy herself. Since Birdie's death, Lulianne had perfected a solo routine that displayed her strengths to their best advantage. Now, she was oblivious to everything except her body moving through the air. She concentrated on her timing, on the control necessary to change quickly from a fast movement to one so slow that it looked to the crowd below as though some invisible hand stilled her.

The performance lasted about ten minutes — not so long

that the crowd picked up on any needless repetitions in her routine and not quite long enough to satisfy them. The first show was a teaser. You wanted the audience to tell their neighbours. You wanted word to go out that there was an airdancer in town. The next day, you wanted the audience jammed tight, lifting the smallest kids up so they had a chance, too, to see the miracle lighting up their drab workaday lives. You wanted, although Lulianne hated the term, to milk the crowd for all they had. So, for each show you added a slightly more spectacular stunt. And each show, with luck, made the audience reach a little deeper into their meagre supply of food or cash.

The teaser gave her enough food to fill her and the great dog for the night, but where could she sleep? Lulianne looked around her. There wasn't anywhere in Tip you could just roll out a swag; it was all shanties and filthy pathways.

'Excuse me,' she said shyly, approaching a woman who was shepherding her children away, 'is there someone round here who'd be willing to shelter me for the night?'

The woman looked at her for such a long time that Lulianne thought she must have not understood her. 'You can come with me,' the woman said finally, 'if you don't mind sharing with the kids.'

'Not at all,' Lulianne said, although she eyed the trio with some trepidation. They looked clean enough. The legs of the eldest were too short for her torso and were bandied, a common enough problem. The middle child was completely bald and his scalp was covered with pale blotches, but he grinned and patted Adri fearlessly. The youngest child was a diminutive girl who had her back turned to Lulianne.

'You can call me Tilley,' the woman said, 'and that one's

Tick, the boy's Ned and this one here's Lovie.' She bent and forced the smaller girl around to face Lulianne.

'But she's beautiful!' Lulianne gasped.

'Oh yes, she's beautiful. A little doll.' The woman took Lulianne's surprise in her stride. 'And you're?'

'Lulianne.' Lulianne offered her hand to the woman who took it and held it for a minute looking at the dark skin before she turned it over, feeling the rope calluses at the base of Lulianne's fingers and thumb. Finally she traced the lines on Lulianne's palm.

'An interesting life,' she said sharply, bringing the hand up closer to her gaze, 'a very interesting life.'

'Haven't we all?' Lulianne felt like snatching her hand away.

'No. Most of us just struggle to do our little bit of living each day. Not you, though. You blaze up, you do. Do you believe me?'

'I don't know,' Lulianne said. 'I don't know what you're doing.'

'Foreseeing. Clairvoyance. Palm reading. I'm good, if you're interested. You have to pay though. And there's no refund if you don't like what I tell you.'

'You reckon you see my future in my hand?'

'I see it, all right.' The woman's fingers traced the lines and whorls on Lulianne's palm. 'A strange one it is with further to go than most of us are able in just one lifetime. You'll make your mark, girl.'

'I don't think so,' Lulianne said, and snatched her hand away. 'I just want somewhere to sleep thanks, no fiddle-faddle.'

'Suit yourself,' Tilley shrugged, 'the offer's open anytime.

10

'The dog'll be all right outside,' she said when they reached her home. 'The place is small enough without that great big thing cluttering it up.'

'Sit, Adri,' Lulianne said, and spread out Adri's sleeping mat before she followed the family inside. Despite Tilley's words the shanty was bigger than many in North Tip. The sleeping area was actually divided from the eating area by a low screen made from woven opaque strips of some kind of plastic. It, and the little brazier which was still glowing with hot coals, made the rough shanty look almost festive.

Tilley pulled out a couple of rough felt mats for the children and presented Lulianne with a large floor cushion. She settled herself down on a crudely made chair, cobbled together from bits of old tubing and more plastic strips. Here was a family, Lulianne thought, who foraged usefully. An old fuel drum even provided them with a table. Apart from that, there was little else in the main room except for some cooking utensils and, most wonderfully and illegally, a small plant growing in a container in one corner.

Lulianne could feel Tilley watching her. She wanted to say something that indicated that, yes, she had seen the plant, and that, no, she wouldn't turn them in.

'It's none of my business,' she said in the end, 'but how does it grow with such little light?'

'I take it out during the day,' Tilley said, still watching. 'I've got some hiding spots. Had it for two years now. It's a bean plant. The first year we were so excited we nearly ate all the beans. Weren't thinking. Weren't thinking about saving the beans, right? Practically on the last mouthful, which Lovie had, of course, I had this thought. So we saved three of them but only one came up. This year we'll do a bit better.'

Lulianne walked over to the plant and touched it. She could already see the baby beans forming. The plant had been carefully tied to a stake and the green tendrils spiralled around it, almost hiding the grey metal.

'It would be lovely even if there weren't any beans,' Lulianne said.

'Gives the room a bit of colour,' Tilley said in her flat voice.

It was true. Everything else in the room was the dull grey or industrial biscuit colour of everything Outside.

'They've got yellow stuff in Glass,' Tick said. She too had been watching Lulianne.

'And blue, like the sky,' her brother said.

'And orange, like the sun,' Lovie smiled at her.

'You've got pink and purple,' Tick said, reaching out but not touching Lulianne's felt performing skirt.

'Dyed specially for me,' Lulianne said, 'in Defence. They've got dyers up there. A bit of cash for a dip.'

'Wish I could go there,' Tick said.

'Wish I could go anywhere,' her brother said.

'I'm staying here with Ma,' Lovie said.

'Well, dreaming doesn't cost anything,' Tilley said, nodding at the children. 'Dreaming's the only thing you can do for nothing, so you keep doing it and stay out of trouble. I've got to go to work now. You look after Lulianne, show her where she can clean up a bit if she wants, and then, Tick, you soak the jerky. We'll have soup when I get in.'

Tick led Lulianne away from the shanty to an open, central public convenience. There was a series of water taps, a latrine dug into the ground and partially screened from passers-by with rough curtains of hessian, and a series of tubs

12

where women were bathing their smaller children and washing clothes.

'You give Old Gran here something if you want some soap.' Tick pointed to an old woman who was sitting beside an older boy with fine dark hair. Lulianne could remember seeing him in the audience. His long, clean hair made him stand out among the other Tip children, although he was no more a child than Lulianne herself was now.

'Or you can bring your own stuff,' Tick continued. ' Me and the kids use sand sometimes. It works just as well.'

Lulianne hadn't had a proper wash since the Circus had played Death. 'I'll get soap,' she said.

'You have to pay her, too, if you want warm water. She tends the fire.'

'I want warm water,' Lulianne said.

'I'll wait for you then,' Tick said, 'in case you can't remember the way home.'

'So you're the airdancer,' the old woman said. 'Welcome to North, lass.'

'Thanks.' Lulianne took some plastic containers from her pack. 'Will these buy me a warm shower and some soap?'

Gran looked the girl slowly up and down. 'Amos here, the brains of Tip,' she said, jerking her head in the boy's direction, 'he said you were lovely up there in the sky. Like a star, he said, a falling star.'

'Thank you.' Lulianne looked directly at Amos and found herself looking into a pair of steady brown eyes, clear of the usual eye infections of Tip.

'You were,' he said. 'Just like a falling star or flower. Made the afternoon bright.'

'So I reckon,' Gran said, 'that we owe you one. Have the

first one on us, lass. Just make sure you return the soap, eh? It's not the best I've seen but it's better'n nothing.'

'Thank you,' Lulianne said, surprised. 'Well, thank you very much.'

The water was lukewarm and the rough soap scraped rather than lathered, but Lulianne washed every bit of herself, even her long dreads. It didn't worry her that little kids, there with their mothers, came to watch her, gaping at the novelty of seeing the airdancer naked. It felt so wonderful to be clean, after the days on the road, the quick dips in cold creeks or rivers, always fearful in case that particular waterway was poisoned.

'You're all shiny,' Tick said as she guided Lulianne home. 'We have a wash only once in a while in winter. Ma says it's too expensive. I'd love to be really clean. We keep Lovie as clean as we can. She's our talisman, Ma says.'

'What does your Ma do?' Lulianne asked, looking down at Tick, who would have been nearly Lulianne's height had her legs been normal.

'She tells fortunes, of course,' Tick said. 'down at Casino. The worker robots play there and when they're winning they want to show off to their women and when they're losing they want her to tell them they're going to win.'

'And do they win?'

'Depends, doesn't it? You can't keep winning,' Tick said. So sometimes Ma gets beaten up. But when she's hot, she's hot and we get lots of cash.'

That explained a lot, Lulianne thought later, as she shared the substantial soup with the family. It explained the better than usual shanty, the relative cleanliness of the children, the spare clothes hanging on a hook in the sleeping area, the felt cushions and even the little bean plant. Ma Tilley could afford these small luxuries. Fortune telling, like any kind of busking, brought in a reasonably regular supply of not only goods but cash, and cash bought what mere bartering could not. Cash bought manufactured items that fell from the back of transports toiling up the highway between Defence, Death and Glass. Cash opened doors and was as scarce as fresh vegetables.

No one got paid cash, though. The few hundred worker robots who lived outside Glass in Rail, a small township of low, narrow buildings hardly much better than Tip, were paid with dope, goods and casino chips. Casino chips were nearly as good as cash, of course, but you had to be lucky. Some were. Some weren't. It was better to be a busker.

Buskers didn't have to go to the daily morning Dump from Glass & Casino to scavenge for things to barter for food. Lulianne had seen the Dump and was grateful that she didn't have to join the jostling crowd who patiently sifted through the rubbish discarded by the Fatters.

For the next four days, Lulianne performed at Tip. She brought back to Tilley's all that she earned. She saved only enough to buy food for Adri to eat. The rest she shared. In the evenings she stayed with the kids while Tilley went to Casino and they played pebble games. The children had carefully stored hoards of pebbles, the favourites, smooth rounds of melted glass or the quartz stones with veins of pink running through them. Wins and losses of these were occasions of triumph and tragedy. Lulianne taught Lovie some clapping games she dimly remembered, even though the girl was really too old to be playing such childish games. Everyone babied Lovie because of her size.

Clap one, clap two, three and four
there's a feral at the door
clap five, clap six, seven and eight
run fast now or it'll be too late
run little one
run, run, RUN!

Or the one Lovie liked best:

Here's to your eyes
both shining bright.
Here's to your arms
both full of might.
Here's to your left
here's to your right
and this one's for the dark,
the dark, black night!

When they were sleepy and lay down together, Lulianne would tell them stories of Circus. She told them about Birdie, leaving out the soldiers, and retelling her death not as a fall but as a last flight.

'And then she just dropped the harness,' Lulianne said, 'and flew, right over the top of the Defence Tower. Right over the top of Defence and everyone watched. We all stood there, our mouths open, as Birdie flew.'

'Tell it again,' Lovie begged. 'Tell us where she grows wings.'

Lulianne had found a new family to replace Circus. She was used to the daily rubbing against other people, the little squabbles and bickering, the good-natured teasing and the secret languages that grew up among people living together in confined spaces, scratching out a meagre communal exis-

tence as best they could, each one dependent on the other
for something.

She kept putting off leaving North Tip.

'You're like another sister,' Tick said to her one night as
they chopped up some carni jerky together to add to the
evening gruel. 'You just fit in here, you know? Ma likes you
just as much as we do, you know that?'

'I like you all, too,' Lulianne said shyly. 'I've never lived
with anyone close to my own age before. It's fun.'

The days settled into a slow rhythm. Tick, Ned and Lovie
always spent some of the day away from Tip, out on
mysterious business of their own, while Lulianne performed
at Casino Market, near the groggers. She grew used to the
constant presence of the white-shirted Security who were
always around and never, unlike the soldiers at Defence, just
part of the crowd. She even grew used to the random erup-
tions of violence from workers strung out on too much dope.

'You should have been there today,' she said, coming
home to Tilley. 'This guy just ran amok and trashed a grog
shop. It took four Security to hold him down. They carted
him off. What do you think would have happened to him?'

'Depends on how much they need him,' Tilley answered.
The older woman was stirring gruel. 'If he was a Div One —
that's a Division One worker with some skills — they will just
cool him down for a couple of days. If he's a Div Five, they'll
probably shoot him.'

'It's awful, isn't it?' Lulianne said, 'this kind of living?'

'It's just life,' Tilley said calmly. 'What else do you want,
girl?'

Tilley reminded Lulianne of Birdie. The children adored
her, and on the nights she worked they all walked her down

17

to Casino Market on the edge of Glass and she would tell them stories of the old days, stories she had heard from her mother who had heard them from her mother. Other kids joined them, including Gran's son, Amos. Tilley's story-telling was well known around North Tip.

'Once,' she said, sweeping her arm in a gesture that took in Tip and Glass and Casino Market, 'once this was covered in a big open city. There were proper shops, not just stalls, and there were offices where people worked. Practically everyone worked and earned cash. It was a golden time, the Golden Age of humankind. There were shops that sold food, big shops as big as Glass itself.'

'As big as Glass?' Lulianne asked. 'I've never heard that before.'

'Oh, it's true. Full of food, all sorts of food. Fresh food, too, not dried. Huge transports went from Defence to Glass, carrying fresh food. And once upon a time Security protected people like us, just ordinary people. They worked for us and so did the government. We paid them — the people paid them and they worked for us and if they weren't any good, they were made to stop working and retire. They were paid to do that, too. Can you imagine it?'

'No,' Lulianne and Tick said in unison.

'Well, it's true. Then there was a huge war. Right across the world which was bigger than just Tip, Death and Defence which is all that's left. Or I think it's all that's left because we never hear about anything else. The Contaminations came, it all changed and we entered the Dark Ages, the Tip Age.'

'That's what I want,' Lulianne said to Tilley, 'a Golden Age. Wouldn't you? I want the old days back when places as big as Glass were full of clothes and food.'

'I want a new Golden Age,' Amos said, limping beside Tilley. When we all wake up and grab back the power. Then we'll have clothes, food and medicine for everyone. Then we can start building a world that goes beyond Glass, beyond everything. We can plant the plants they've got caged up inside Glass. We can make everything green again.'

'Sshh, Amos. Talk like that invites trouble. We don't want any trouble.'

'We've got trouble already, Tilley. How many children starve? How many people die because we haven't medicine? Why can't we have what they've got in there, in Glass? Why are we outside while they're inside? Why shouldn't Glass belong to all of us?'

'Because that's what happened,' Tilley said. 'That's what happened after the Contaminations. You know that, Amos.'

*   *   *

One night Tilley didn't come home. The children's restless stirrings, as though without their mother's hushed nightly return deep sleep evaded them, woke Luliannne. Then Lovie cried out in a dream and grabbed the older girl's hand, so she had to gently shake herself free from the child's tight grip.

Lulianne rolled away from the squirming children and got up, shivering in the sudden cold. It was never quite dark outside Glass, but the sky was lightening in the East and the Casino would have closed some time ago to allow the workers just enough time to get some sleep before the morning shift. Tilley should have been home. She should have been either sleeping on the other side of the children or lighting the small chip fire for the morning porridge and tea.

Lulianne stepped outside. Already there was stirring

19

around North but these familiar sights didn't catch Lulianne's attention. Instead she focused on two figures struggling up West Path, dragging something behind them.

A small hand slipped into Lulianne's. She looked down and saw Lovie.

'It's Ma,' the girl said, 'come on.' And she let go of Lulianne's hand and darted towards the path.

It *was* Tilley who the two men were dragging.

'Dumped for dead,' the older man said, 'just out past the Casino.'

'She's not though,' the boy said. 'Still breathing, see?'

They stood and watched Tilley's chest rise slightly and fall. She whimpered, faintly, and Lovie, standing beside Lulianne, gave an answering whimper, the way a pup might call to its mother.

'Been good to us, has Tilley,' the man said, 'otherwise we'd have left her.'

'Missed the Dump,' the boy said. 'Supposed to be cans on this one and all.'

'Can you bring her home?' Lulianne asked. 'I couldn't get her up there by myself.'

'You take over from Stev,' the man said. 'Stev, you head back. Might still be some salvage.'

Together Lulianne and the man hauled Tilley up the rest of the way. Lovie stripped off her own tunic to wrap around her mother's bleeding feet to protect them from the rough gravel.

'Doesn't matter, child,' the man said, but with real sadness in his voice, 'she can't hardly feel a thing, you know.'

Lovie said nothing, just wrapped her arms around her scrawny, naked torso.

'Up we go then.'

Lulianne could hardly look at Tilley's head. The left side was caked with blood but underneath the matted hair a bruised lump had already formed. Her eyes were swollen closed and her nose was askew on her face.

'Better get Gran,' the man said when they'd lowered Tilley down onto the sleeping mat. 'The water woman and that boy. They did her last time. Wasn't as bad as this, mind. This'll take magic, I reckon.'

The children stood around as though reluctant to move away from their mother, until Tick prodded Ned and he went off. He seemed not to realise he was crying, just brushed away the tears as he went, as though they were summer flies. Lulianne felt her own eyes fill with tears as she watched him run down to the water square.

'Gor,' Gran said when she arrived with Amos, 'she's done it this time. Someone hit her too hard. You got water, girl? Heat some up and let's see what's under this mess.'

Amos and the old woman worked together, examining Tilley gently, spreading a smelly ointment on the cuts and bruises, packing Tilley's nose in a rough splint made from foraged plastic strips. They finally propped up the woman and spilled something from a small plastic bottle into her mouth.

Lulianne admired the way Amos handled Tilley so gently, even though the woman was past feeling a thing. She wasn't good with the sick. Her earliest memories were of holding the sick bucket for her mother, washing her sores and banging her thin back so the woman would cough up the choking phlegm. To even think of it now made her practically dry retch. She controlled herself, though, because it was almost a treat to see Amos working so precisely, his fingers sure as he

21

dabbed and swabbed. It was a change to see the rabble-rouser Amos, with his constant questions and commentary, turn back to healer.

When they finished, he laid the groaning Tilley back down.

'She'll need more of this in the morning,' Gran said, giving the small plastic bottle to Lulianne, 'and put more of this on her eye. That's a bad split but that's not the worst of it. The real killer is infection and we can't prevent that here. Either she's strong enough or she isn't. That's Tip story. And in there' — she motioned in the city's direction — 'they've medicine that heals instantly. Imagine that. Out here children fall and scrape and the next day they're alight with fever, while in there, pah!' She made a spitting sound. 'Come on boy, got to go.'

'Will she be all right?' Lulianne asked Amos as he lingered behind Gran.

'Not going anywhere in a hurry,' Amos said. He touched the girl's shoulder and she noticed how smooth his hands were, compared with her calloused ones. 'We'll do our best, eh, Airdancer? That's all we can do. Gran's right, though, they've everything we need in Glass. Time to go in and get it, eh?'

Lulianne stared after the boy and the old woman and wondered what his last words meant.

Clan is all we have. Clan comes before each and everyone of us and is each and everyone of us. The Aunties tell us what is good for Clan because to be chosen as an Aunty you have to have seen life and gained wisdom, but even they will listen to opinions and ideas other than their own, because not one person or one group of people can ever be Clan. Clan is bigger than all of us but belongs to us all.

Auntie Teece, Clan

Egan left the Soltram at Nine, pulled the vehicle off the old railway track and hid it in some low scrub, not that anyone would find it this far out of Glass and the Tips. Feral killings made all the districts off Main dangerous and few people ventured out here, but the Aunties had made a charm against the big cats. If it failed, well, there was always an arrow nocked and ready for any feral cat that thought Egan might be good pickings! They hunted mainly at night — only a tough Dry would see them hunting in the morning sun — so it was easy to stride out, whistling, alert to noises but not too worried.

It was a two-day hike even with the Soltram, but there were always things to see and hear and a dilly bag at the ready for any new plants or small animals. Last Full there were frog noises all along Winding Creek: a good thing, Aunty Teece had said. Meant the water was running clean. The old Aunties had celebrated that. It was the furthest down the Winding frogs had been heard. He'd seen a couple — funny looking hoppers, made him laugh. He'd imagined they'd be miraculous, the way the Aunties talked, but they were just slime-coloured, wet looking things, all self-important throat and long jumping legs.

This time, snakes were sunbaking on the rocks in the middle of the Winding. Two of them lay coiled together, although he'd thought it was one at first. It was late for anything to be mating but snakes liked it hotter. There were snakes up at Clan — you watched where you walked in the hot months, but this was the first time he had seen them this close to the denuded Main. They were big ones, too, three times as thick as a man's arm — and a muscled Clan man, at that, not a skinny under-nourished Tipper.

Who'd live in Tip? Egan didn't understand it. Sure, it was busy, it hustled. There were things to scavenge. There was Casino, the groggers, the Market, but there was also stench and noise, the depressing ever-present hunger, and the mean grubby lives. Above it all, Glass, a reminder of everything you didn't have. Everything soft and clean, patrolled endlessly by white-shirted Security. Most Tippers didn't believe in Clan, that was the trouble. And the ones that did, like Tilley?

'Our life's here, boy. I was born in Tip, my kids were born in Tip. We're used to Tip.'

'But Tilley, there's real life in Clan.'

'There's life here, Egan, look around you. What do you call it?'

Egan called it living death but he knew better than to say that to Tilley. The Aunties said anyone was welcome into Clan but they didn't say to go out and get people, either.

'Tip will change,' Tilley told him, 'the Fatters are getting old. We just need a bit of patience, Egan, and then Glass and

24

everything they have will be ours. We get by, Egan, we do okay.'

Tilley and her kids did okay, Egan had to admit. But the rest of the Tippers? The hustlers, the scroungers, yeah, they did well, if all you wanted at the end of the day was to drink voddy, play some losing numbers, go to bed to get up and do it all over again with hangover. On the other hand, you could say that Clan was always the same, too. Dig the garden, weed the garden, plant the garden, send out rain charms, go to bed to get up and do it all over again. He was lucky going to Tip to do a little bartering and pick up the gossip. The Aunties liked getting news of Tip, and certain people in Tip liked getting news of the Aunties. A bit of both worlds was good, you couldn't get bored then, couldn't think you were missing out on too much.

Egan pulled out the bone pipes he carried with him and blew a new tune, about walking along in the quietness of the low scrub. Strange that music could be about quietness. It sounded a little wistful. Was he lonely? Sometimes the pipes caught at something deep in your heart, too deep for you to really know it was there until the pipes sang it out. And today, they weren't just singing about aloneness, they were singing about loneliness.

'That's not what I meant,' he said, shaking them slightly as though to dislodge any remnant of sadness from the bleached bones.

'I want a holiday song,' he said. 'I'm on holidays from the garden, don't you get it?' The pipes remained mute. They knew. They always did. They'd caught a melancholy restlessness in him. It had been there for a while like a chilly wind that blew up from nowhere on the sunniest day, catching him out at odd times, when he should have been concentrating on something else — hunting, or planting, or just walking — making him think too much about things that were unanswerable. He wondered why he was alive, why things were the way they were and, most of all, why he was alone.

He blew the pipes again, changing their notes, making them skip along the way the Winding did. The pipes obeyed this new call, the notes tumbled in a pleasing rush of busyness, one after another, leaving no room for the loneliness he had heard before. But when he stopped playing, the silence seemed bigger.

'Oh, get away with you,' he said and stuffed them back in his pack. Better to just walk. Better to walk and look around. Concentrate on the outside — count clouds, birds, insects, anything to fill that little hollow of emptiness inside.

Before the sun was centred in the sky, he'd reached the outskirts of North Tip, ash and refuse drifting on the hot breeze. Too early to walk in, really — it paid to be careful and not draw too much attention to yourself. He scouted around and found a safe place, an ideal place with a clear view of Tip.

The sun dazzled off the walls of Glass and there was a faint, but persistent insect drone from clouds of small black flies. Time to hunker down and rest — there was nothing else to do. A couple of hours wait would take the glare out of the day, lengthen the shadows and make his approach to Tip less obvious. He didn't mean to doze off but the flies' lullaby and the warmth of the sun conspired to make him sleep.

'I'll get that bitch,' someone very close swore. 'By Contamination, I'll get her.'

Egan woke with a jerk. He grabbed for his knife, cursing silently. How could he have been so stupid? He could be killed

26

from sheer carelessness. Cautiously he eased around, shielded by the scrub, the shadows and the walls of the mound he'd slept in. A man, only a few metres away, standing up in plain view, swigged on a bottle of voddy. Talk about careless! Egan couldn't believe his eyes. The man stood out in the desolate landscape like a forest tree.

'Contaminated bitch,' he shouted, waving his fists at the sky. 'I'll get her if I have to drag her back by her hair.'

What would make a man drunk and raving at midday? The Aunties would say voddy was enough by itself. But was it? Egan edged back, deeper into the hollows of the mound, careful not to touch the dirt walls. If it all collapsed he'd be well and truly exposed. Some of the mounds weren't as calcified as others and it was better to be cautious.

The man tripped suddenly, only just saving himself — and the voddy. Then he sat down anyway, mumbling and raving to himself between swigs. Just watching him guzzle down the voddy made Egan thirsty. A little bit of voddy could open the world a crack wider and let some new stars into your life. But when you got bad voddy or simply too much — that was different. You could be buzzed awake, jumpy and even downright scared for hours, until finally the drug left your system and you could sleep again.

Egan thought of his still bubbling back at Clan. The Aunties didn't know about that — they were against voddy.

'Brainrot,' Aunty Teece said. 'Dissolves your brain cells and turns you into a puppet for the Fatters, that's all voddy does. Disgusting stuff.'

On the other hand, Egan and his friends thought a little bit of good voddy used to celebrate a good hunt or a good season or new life in Clan added a warm glow that tea just couldn't give you.

'Okay Nem, we're going to get her! We're going in. Contaminate her! We're going to drag her back half-dead if we have to. We don't care a Contamination but we won't be kicked over by some trouble-making girl we paid for, we bought fair and square. She's our property, Circus stock. And we're going to get her back.'

Property, then — except that this property seemed to be a person. Well, it was true then, you could trade anything in some places. That was creepy.

The man stood up unsteadily and hurled the empty bottle. An itinerant, obviously — bottles were expensive. Rule of Clan, rule of Tip, never chuck anything away. If you did, you were either mad or travelling light, travelling too light. Egan noted the bottle landed in a group of small bushes, about a handspan away from a mound. He should find that easily.

'Get going,' he urged the traveller in his mind, 'scram!'

Egan wanted to be hustling. He shifted restlessly in his hiding spot. Curse the drunk! He was slower than a rainy day. As soon as the stranger moved, lurching towards Tip, Egan was off.

When he found the bottle, he let out a low whistle. Still half a swig left! What kind of waster threw that away? Without a pause Egan upended the bottle and swallowed.

'Whoa!' he spluttered. 'Good stuff.'

It was eye-wateringly strong. He'd never had anything like that before. Where did it come from? It should have a warning on the bottle. It was the kind of voddy that gave the drink a bad name, the sort that could make you blind. It was a wonder the guy was still standing, let alone walking. A good thing there had only been a bit left — any more and Egan would have had to sit down and recover.

He set off cautiously on high alert, doubling back over his tracks, zigzagging through the low scrub. No rogue Security high on dope was going to get him. Sweat dripped into his eyes and stung his face. His hamstrings and shoulders ached. There wasn't much vegetation so close to Tip and Glass but every bit of it was hostile. Clumps of sword grass slashed stinging cuts in legs and arms, and huge thistles grabbed at anything they could. If all that didn't get you, the ticks would.

'Contaminated things,' Egan swore to himself, stopping to pull another one from his leg. They burrowed through anything for flesh. It was easy to just pick off the fat, blood-engorged belly but then the pincered head would keep mechanically pumping poison. Everyone had a story of someone keeling over, nothing apparently wrong with them, until the discovery of that telltale lump concealing the vicious little head, putrid and deadly.

Where the mounds clumped together, Egan managed a good pace, and by the time the Security Tower was in sight he'd practically caught up with the drunk who had slowed down and become more cautious as Tip loomed closer. The smell was worse now — it took a couple of days of Tip to get used to it. There was the Tower all right — and his drunken friend. But what was going on up there? Why were there so many people around and what were they looking at?

'Contaminations!' Egan couldn't help the word escaping. There, way up on the cross beam nearly at the very top of the tower was a figure that made him gasp. It was dressed in bright colours that blazed against the sky. He'd never seen such colours, not even in the garden. He'd never seen such hot, wonderful colours. And then, while he was looking, the person up there, stepped into the air and began to fall. He started forward and stopped, as the air seemed to grab the figure and spin it in dizzying circles before it somersaulted over and over, the colours tumbling like petals in the wind. Egan gasped.

It was beautiful. He crawled as close as he dared and nearly bumped into the drunk.

'There the bitch is,' the man slurred as though to Egan. 'She's there. She can't do that by herself. She's Circus not a solo act. Bitch. I'll get her.' He staggered forward.

So that *was* the story. The busker belonged to the drunk somehow, or he thought she did. He'd paid for her and she'd scarpered.

* * *

The girl descended, each somersault slower and more deliberate than the last. Egan held his breath, even though he knew now that she must be harnessed. When she reached the ground he wanted her to climb up and do it all again. The way she stepped into the air as though she stepped into safe arms, the calculated fall and then the turning over and over, like a flower, like a wish falling to earth, was the loveliest thing he had ever seen in his life.

Children ran out to her, and who was that with her? It was Amos. Amos was there. What was going on in Tip? Who the Contamination was she? Her hair was a mass of coloured dreads, the same colours as her clothes, and he could almost smell her on the air, a musky perfume undercutting the usual Tip smells of mildew, rubbish and decay.

30

Then the drunk moved out into the open, the girl yelled something and the kids all clustered around, ruining his view. Something was going on. Egan half stood up, trying to see. The drunk was pulling at the girl.

'That waster!' He couldn't bear to think of her belonging to the brutal drunk.

Don't go with him. He sent the thought winging through the air towards the crowd of children. *Don't go with him. He's not good enough for you.*

He should go down. He fingered his knife. There was a lot of yelling but dust rose up around the group and concealed all the action. Blast it. Egan started loping down the hill.

He had waited too long. By the time he'd made his way down, the dust had cleared , the drunk was groaning on the ground, clutching his knee and the kids had moved off. Egan joined the huddle of children and was carried along with them.

They were laughing and reliving the blows they'd struck.

'He can't have you,' said a girl Egan recognised. 'We'll protect you, Lulianne.'

So that was her name. Lulianne. The name made your tongue feel happy. Lulianne. Where did she come from? What was she doing in North Tip? The brightly dyed felt skirt she wore was like a flag — no wonder the children followed her. She was the brightest thing he had ever seen. Made you grin, those colours blaring against the grimy grey. The way she walked, too, stepping high, as proud and confident as a young pacca. She was more Clan than Tip. She made his heart somersault, slowly, the way she had tumbled in the air. What would the Aunties make of her? Would they finger the felt of her skirt enviously or in disdain?

Egan shook his head crossly. The Aunties would say he'd fallen in lust. The Aunties didn't know everything. He had never seen anyone like this Lulianne. Thank the skies she hadn't gone with that stupid drunk but what was she doing walking so comfortably next to Amos? Amos had his causes. He didn't have time for a girl. But a girl and a garden! They went together well. There was dawdling time in a garden and shady places to loiter and, oh shut up, you fool!

Still, a girl like that belongs in a garden. This thought put a bounce in Egan's step as he walked behind the children, into North.

You can't heal a body that doesn't want to heal, no matter what medicine or magic you use. Gran told me that and she was right. People's lives slipped out of our grasp because they didn't want to keep living. Their lives lurched from one voddy to the next, one game of dice to the next. They had nothing else. It wasn't enough. We needed hope. That's what made us want to live, made us want to see the sun come up the next morning. It was that simple.

from *The Lessons of Amos from North Tip,*
Healer and Revolutionary

Tilley was worse the next day, despite Lulianne's night vigil. She wandered in and out of consciousness, delirious, her forehead was searingly hot. When Gran came with Amos she tutted and examined the long reddening gash near Tilley's eye.

'Infection,' she muttered. 'Could be bad.'

'She has to get better!' Tick said, 'She has to Gran. What about us?'

'Oh, she wants to get better — feel her head girl, feel that heat? That's her body fighting back.'

The children crowded around their mother's bed, and although Lulianne tried to bribe them away with offers of porridge they refused to budge, until Gran said, 'You're taking all her air. Scram, kids. Hey, Lulu get them out of here, will you? You go too, Amos. Scat, all of you.'

They left reluctantly.

'What am I going to do?' Lulianne implored Amos. 'What does she want me to do?'

But the boy was already ahead of her, clapping his hands

33

together and calling out, 'Circus lessons with the airdancer of Glass. C'm on kids, free circus lessons with Lulianne, airdancer of Glass.'

'What?'

'Free circus lessons! Join the airdancer of Glass for your free circus lesson!' Amos called, and a crowd of children emerged from every nook and cranny of Tip and followed them.

'I don't do free anything,' Lulianne said.

'There's always a first time,' Amos grinned at her. 'Anyway, come on, it'll take their minds off it.'

The kids gathered around the old Security Tower and Lulianne and Amos began. It was easier than Lulianne thought it would be. Yes, they all wanted to learn, and some were agile and determined and tackled the tasks she set as though proving something important, but to whom she was uncertain. Themselves? Or maybe Amos? Everyone knew Amos, of course, but some of the children seemed to know him particularly well and worked together in small, tight groups. These were the ones who kept at a trick or move until they could do it perfectly. They helped each other, Lulianne noticed, with encouraging words and gestures. They were like Circus without being Circus and made her feel oddly homesick. Ned, Tilley's boy, moved straight into a group like this and Lulianne wondered if he was involved with one of the girls in it, a girl called Burr who was tall and apparently fearless. When they'd learned what they wanted to, they set out helping the littlies.

Amos, who, surprisingly, brought some juggling balls out of one of his capacious pockets, proved to be an able teacher in his own right, although Lulianne was taken aback by his teaching methods. 'These are the Fatters in Glass,' he said, holding up the balls, 'so if you drop them, drop them hard!' His students giggled and some of them deliberately dropped the balls or banged them hard together when it was their turn.

The morning passed quickly and the children only straggled back to their dingy homes when their empty bellies told them it was lunchtime. Even then a few lingered and Lulianne knew they must be strays.

'Shoo,' Amos said mildly, 'go on, you'll miss begging if you hang round here. We don't have anything for you.'

'Thanks, Amos,' one scabby little boy said. 'Thanks for the juggling.'

'Come back later,' Amos said, 'and we'll learn some more.'

'What do you mean by that?' Lulianne asked him when the strays had wandered off.

'Tilley's in for a hard time,' Amos said. 'She's not getting better in a hurry. May as well do this to keep those kids occupied, don't you think? It was a bit of fun, all right. Wasn't it?'

'Sure,' Lulianne said. 'But I've got a living to make. I'm not some freebie teacher.'

'The kids loved it,' Amos said, his eyes steady on her. 'Gave them a taste of something bigger than all this and they felt they belonged. They'll need that if they're ever going to fight against this.'

Lulianne kept her eyes resolutely on the muddy track they were following back to Gran's. Beside them, the abject shanties, held together with spit and will, shifted in the slight breeze that also wafted the pungent mix of decaying rubbish, mildew and disease into the air.

'The kids are our future,' Amos continued. 'They can change everything.'

'Nothing changes.' Lulianne was drawn in despite herself. 'But at least we're not worker robots.'

'Everything changes, all the time,' Amos said. 'Change is happening all around us. Think the Fatters live forever? They don't. Not for all their carni culture and fresh greens. They've gotta die, just like we have to. And there are some people who would hurry that along, given half a chance.'

'Are you one of them?' Lulianne asked, catching a note in his voice.

'Of course,' Amos said. 'Anyone with any sense is. Aren't you?'

Lulianne shrugged. 'There were people like you in Defence,' she said. 'They got shot.'

'There are lots of us, Lulianne, just biding our time. They can't shoot us all.'

'Can't they? They can do anything they want. You know that.'

Despite her protests, Lulianne found herself teaching more children that afternoon.

Halfway through the lesson, Lulianne saw a familiar figure lurking around the shanties to the left of the tower.

'This is my turf, Nemrick,' she shouted. 'Find your own place!'

Nemrick sauntered out. 'What's this?' he jeered. 'Circus tryouts?'

Lulianne looked around and saw the scene through his eyes, the scabby, dirty children, most, no doubt, louse- and worm-ridden. A couple you looked at and knew that death was already knocking on their door: that little girl, clumsily dropping Amos's juggling balls, with her caved-in chest, so thin that there was scarcely a breath width between her front and back ribs, and the boy no one would play with, his features blunted, already eroding with the onset of the Numbing Disease.

'Get out of here, Nemrick. This is my turf, I told you.'

'Come on, Lulianne, you don't belong here. Come back with me, come back where you belong.'

'I'm solo now, Nemrick. I'm never coming back. You know why.'

'I was drunk on voddy, Lulu. It won't happen again.'

'That's what you said the last time, and the time before that.'

'So what. So what if we cosy up together. You're telling me that would be worse than this?' Nemrick laughed. 'Take a good look, Lulianne, and then tell me you'd prefer to be here than with me.'

Behind her, Lulianne could sense the children listening. Amos pushed himself forward to stand beside her.

'Your new man, eh?' Nemrick said. 'Old Leaner here?'

'Just get out,' Lulianne said. 'I choose to stay here. At least I can do that. You don't let me choose. You'd take me by force, whatever it took. This is my family now.'

'You'll choose me by the time I'm through with you, you tight-arsed little scrag. Come here, you're coming home.' Nemrick stepped forward, and as he did Adri leapt with bristling fur and bared teeth to fill the space between the man and the girl.

'Get down,' Nemrick shouted and went to swipe the dog out of the way. Adri, avoiding the man's flesh, grabbed his sleeve.

'Bloody dog, get down,' Nemrick kicked at the dog.

'Stop it, Nemrick. I'm not going. Down Adri. Leave him alone.'

The dog let go abruptly, unbalancing the man who lurched forward and grabbed Lulianne. Adri crouched growling, waiting for the girl's orders.

'Let her go,' Amos said, his voice level.

'What are you going to do about it, Leaner?' Nemrick had forced Lulianne's arm behind her back. He could, they both knew, break it. Still she didn't set Adri on him.

'Let her go. She's chosen us, not you.'

'You lot of gimps and poxers, no clear thinker would choose you. You must have addled her brains with some of your dope.'

'Let Lulianne go.' It was Lovie who spoke this time, walking up to stand by Amos. Her miniature fists were clenched.

'And who are you, beauty. Might take you as well, eh? You'd draw a crowd, I reckon. The Living Doll. Eats, breathes and even talks. Yeah, I reckon you'd be a little earner.'

Nemrick lunged towards Lovie, but as he reached for her Amos struck him hard, surprising the man.

'Contaminations! Putting up a fight, eh?' Nemrick said, quickly gaining his balance. He circled Amos, keeping Lulianne between them as though using her as a shield. Amos circled with him, waiting for the older man to leave himself unguarded.

Lovie threw the first stone. She raised one small fist and the stone flew beautifully from her hand and hit Nemrick on the knee-cap. It was not a large stone, but it stung and Nemrick loosened his grip on Lulianne, who twisted away, calling Adri as she did.

'Out, girl, out!'

'Let her go.' Amos shouted. 'Let the dog get him.'

Stones were flying now. The children had armed themselves. They were hurling stones, sticks, bits of old tin and anything they could find at Nemrick who seemed stunned by their unexpected attack. He stood there gobsmacked for a moment and then tried, impotently, to protect himself with his arms.

'I can't,' Lulianne said. 'She'll tear him to bits. Get out, Nemrick, go before you're really hurt, you old fool, go!'

A large stone, thrown with more force than the others, hit Nemrick on the side of his head and he crumpled to the ground, moaning.

'Call your bloody army off,' he said, rocking back and forth, holding his head in his hands. 'Call your midgets off, you bitch.'

He was cut and bleeding, bruises already purpling on his face and arms. His clothes were torn and he looked very different from the man who had sauntered in ready to claim his own.

The children clustered around. One or two kicked him, one in the ribs, the other aiming for his balls.

'That'll learn you to call us gimps and poxers,' one of the boys said and then spat.

'We don't want to see you here again,' Amos said, leaning forward and speaking right in Nemrick's face. 'Do you get that, old man. If we see you here again, we'll kill you. Got it? Right out of Glass, we mean. Got it? We've got kids everywhere, East, South and West, so don't try anything.'

'We've no cash,' Nemrick whimpered. 'And it's not just me, it's the others, too. And the dogs.'

Lulianne fished around under her top for her cash pouch.

'Don't give him anything,' Amos said. 'He tried to round you up, don't you know?'

'He's nearly my father,' Lulianne said, throwing some cash down at Nemrick. 'And there are the dogs. I grew up with them. That'll be enough Nemrick, if you and the others don't buy voddy or morph. If you're clean, that'll get you back to Death. Cash is good there. You'll get enough to last you until Defence.'

'Don't want to go back to Defence. Don't want to go back to Birdie's ashes.'

'Can't stay here,' Amos said, 'because we'll kill you.' And the children moved in closer. Some of them still had stones in their hands.

'All right.' Nemrick got up on his hands and knees. 'Ahh, I think you've broken my bloody leg!'

Amos looked at him with professional interest. 'No,' he said, 'that'd be where Lovie got you the first time. Possibly a chipped knee-cap, that's all.'

'I can't walk.'

'Crawl then,' Amos said. 'Come on, kids, time to pack up.'

Lulianne went with the others. She didn't look back at Nemrick. She knew she would never see him again.

'I owe you,' she said to Amos and Lovie as they walked over to Tilley's.

'The dog would have got him, if you'd let her.'

'He'd have hurt her.'

'That wasn't why you wouldn't let her. You were scared.'

'I was,' Lulianne said. 'I was scared of what she could do to him.'

'You can't afford that kind of fear,' Amos said.

'Oh come on, Amos,' Lulianne, touching his shoulder, 'you wouldn't have killed him. Nemrick's stupid, not evil.'

'So you'd have gone with him rather than kill him?'

It was late afternoon and the light was a sickly lemon colour, picking up from the reflectors of Glass. In that light even Lovie looked ill. Lulianne reached down to pat Adri and hide her face.

'Would you have just gone with him?'

'I don't think I could have killed him,' Lulianne answered slowly, her fingers holding on to the dog's rough fur. 'You don't understand. He let me ride on his shoulders when I was a kid. He and Birdie swung me between them on the long walks. We shared our food.'

'No, you're right, I don't understand.' Amos shrugged. 'He's practically your father but he's willing to rape you and you'd just let him, a bullying bastard like that? What's the matter with you?'

'I didn't let him rape me.' Lulianne looked up, glaring. 'I ran away. I didn't think he'd come after me.'

'I'm glad we were there,' Amos said gently. 'We don't harbour scruples like you. Kids from Tip kill if we have to.'

'So you saved me and I owe you, but you wouldn't have killed him. You're a healer, not a murderer.'

'I'm whatever is necessary,' the boy said, and something metal in his voice made Lulianne lean away from him. 'I do whatever it takes. We all will when it comes to it. We'll all have to.'

It was whispered around Tip that the Airdancer of Glass and her army had beaten a giant who'd come to town to round her up. It was whispered around North Tip and from

41

there to the other Tips where rumours made the one giant many and the army grow steadily.

We'd like to think everyone could live like Clan — and they could. In Tip, though, and in Glass, there's no community. Everyone fights for themselves, not for each other. We don't ask what Clan does for us. We ask what we do for Clan.

Aunty Teece, Clan

Egan was curious when the airdancer and Amos headed for Tilley's shanty. He wasn't at all sure that he wanted to meet the girl while Amos was with her. So he headed up to the Water Square where he hoped to find Gran and catch up on the gossip.

The old woman was sitting at her post. 'Egan,' she said nodding, although he hadn't even noticed her look up at him.

'Gran,' he said, 'how's things in the water business?'

'Slow,' Gran said, 'but things are worse for some. Have you heard about Tilley?'

'No. I came straight here,' Egan said, sitting down on a lump of stone next to Gran.

'Tilley was bashed. Badly.'

'She's all right?'

Gran shrugged. 'Not getting better in a hurry,' she said. 'You got some of your magic oil with you?'

'Yeah, I've got some, but it's not magic, you know.'

'We'll try anything. Let's go.'

'Who is the busker?' Egan asked as they walked over together. 'Where did she come from?'

'Calls herself Lulianne. Just turned up one day with her little bag of tricks. Don't know where she came from. Bit of colour, though. The kids and Amos think she's all right. Staying with Tilley. Good thing someone is.'

'Yeah, I noticed. She was giving lessons. They were interrupted, though, by some bloke giving her a hard time. Amos and the kids sorted him.'

'Don't know anything about him,' Gran said. 'Ask her yourself if you're interested. You won't be able to stay at Tilley's though. It's too crowded and she's too sick. You'll have to bunk in with Amos.'

They could hardly all fit inside the shanty and Amos shooed the kids out of the way. 'You don't know how glad I am to see you, Egan,' he said. 'Have you got that oil with you? It could be our last hope.'

'That's Tilley?' exclaimed Egan as he approached the pallet on which the sick woman lay.

'Not looking her best,' Gran said.

Tilley's eyes were shut. The sound of laboured breathing rasped and already the air smelled different, a hot, sticky smell. One side of the woman's face was badly bruised and the cut glared above her eye, oozing pus from the corner.

Egan handed the bottle over. 'Use all of it, Amos, don't spare any. By Contamination, who could do such a thing?'

'Some angry punter,' Gran said. 'She's hot, Amos. She's burning up.'

'Bathe her.' Amos opened the bottle and sniffed its pungent contents gratefully. 'Bathe her wrists, that might cool her down a bit.'

'I could get water.' The girl stepped forward. Up this close she wasn't as beautiful as Egan had imagined. The skin under her eyes was crisscrossed with fine lines, as though she'd spent a lot of time squinting into the sun, and that made her look older. There was a sternness about her that surprised him, but he was relieved she wasn't beautiful. It would have been too much.

'I'll come with you,' he said. 'You must be feeling a bit shaken after what happened with that man.'

'Did you see it?' Lulianne asked as they set off up to the Water Square.

'Yeah. I came down from … I came into Glass today behind him. He was pretty mad.'

'You came from Defence?'

There was a quick curiosity in the girl's voice and she looked him over more closely now, taking in his clothes and his appearance for the first time.

'Not Defence,' he said, 'just Outside.'

'That's a good cloak you've got,' Lulianne said, fingering it. He saw her strong fingers and square-palmed hands. 'I haven't seen that kind of felt here,' she continued, looking straight ahead rather than at Egan. 'Or in Defence. Must be pretty special. Must have cost a lot.'

'Warm though,' Egan said. He didn't want to lie to Lulianne. He liked the way she walked with him, lengthening her strides to match his. But he didn't want to tell her the truth, either. Not until he knew more about her. The Aunties wouldn't be proud of him if they thought he'd gabbled about Clan to a stranger.

'What's the oil?' she asked.

'A healing oil. It's good but I reckon it'll have a hard time with Tilley. She's pretty far gone.'

'Do you think she'll die?'

'Guess so. Couldn't you smell it?'

Lulianne shook her head. 'Smell what?'

'That smell around her? That hot, sweetish smell?'

'I thought it was just — you know — Tip?'

'No, not that smell. This is different. It's death, if you're not very lucky.'

'The children,' Lulianne said, 'what will happen to them? They've had it okay, you know. Tilley is a good mother. They've had enough food and even medicine when they needed it. What will happen to Lovie?'

'I could take them home with me,' Egan said without thinking, 'if they want to come.'

'Where's home?'

'Oh just … look, here we are. I'll pump first, you hold the bucket.' He was pleased to evade the question.

When the bucket was half-full, they swopped jobs.

'It looks pretty bad,' Egan said, examining the grey scummy water.

'Normal,' Lulianne said. 'The washing water's worse. It's all their run-off,' and Egan followed her head-jerk towards Glass. She stopped pumping and wiped the sweat from her forehead.

'Ever been inside?'

'No.' Egan said. 'Don't want to, either. Gives me the heebie-jeebies, that place. I like being out in the air.'

'I know what you mean. So where is home, mister fresh air?'

'Look, it doesn't matter, right? The main thing is to get this to Tilley. I'll tell you another time.'

'You can trust me, you know. Tilley has.'

'I'm sure I can.' He picked up the bucket but the girl grabbed half the handle.

'No need to wear yourself out. I don't mind a bit of hard yakka, you know. I'm Circus. We're used to it.'

'You're a flyer, aren't you?'

'An airdancer.' The girl straightened her neck and back.

'An airdancer,' he repeated, 'it sounds so … free.'

'It isn't though, not really. You've got these harnesses.'

'It sounds free,' Egan said stubbornly.

They walked back to Tilley's in silence. Egan watched her from the corner of his eye. Her arms were fined down to muscle and bone and the weight of the bucket didn't trouble her. They made a good couple, he thought, but Lulianne wasn't even looking at him. She lengthened her stride when they came in sight of Tilley's hut and the movement sent the water splashing in the bucket.

'Watch it,' she said to Egan.

'I didn't do that.'

'Well, watch it anyway.'

The hut smelt different when they got back. It was the oil.

'Amazing stuff,' Amos said. 'I've used most of it, Egan.'

'Keep it,' Egan said, 'you'll probably need the rest.'

Amos nodded. 'What exactly is it?' he asked.

Egan jerked his head a fraction towards Lulianne. It was okay for everyone else to trust the airdancer and he wanted to, but he was still smarting from her snappiness over the water. Anyway, he didn't want to be tricked into trusting her just because he thought she was beautiful and made him want to touch her.

'You can trust Lulianne,' Amos said. 'She's one of us, aren't you?'

'Of course I am,' Lulianne said, 'and Circus don't blab. We're close, Circus, we have to be.'

'She's been looking after the kids, Egan,' Amos said. 'She's stayed on to help since Tilley was bashed. She's part of Tip, as well as Circus. She's one of us.'

'I just don't think the Aunties would …'

'Oh, don't be daft, young fellow,' Gran said. 'For heaven's sake, Egan, what's got into you? Just tell the story, boy.'

Egan felt himself blushing. It wasn't fair. The one time he was being careful and everyone was down on him.

'All right,' he muttered, 'if you say so.' He pulled up an old box and sat down on it. Lulianne crouched between him and Amos, who was helping Gran sponge-bath Tilley.

'We found it by accident,' Egan said. 'Just one of those lucky things. One of the Aunties liked the smell of the plant. She said it reminded her of something she'd smelled way back — she was the daughter of a survivor. She put it on a burn. Just rubbed it on, straight from the leaf, you know. The burn healed really quickly. So then we started thinking. We distilled the oil from it, used it, and it worked.'

'Where do you come from?' Lulianne asked. 'Why the big secret?'

Egan jerked his head roughly in the direction of the mountains. 'Up there,' he said.

Lulianne peered out of the doorway in disbelief.

'Up in the *mountains*? So it's true, then?' She laughed.

'What?'

'When we were in Defence there was always talk about people who'd escaped somehow, who weren't living in Defence or Death or Glass. They said there were tribes of ferals, living like animals, all over, they said. You didn't travel outside Defence at night in case they got you. Mothers used to tell their kids to come home before dark or the mountain people would get you, eat you and hang your skull on a post.'

Egan snorted. 'We're nothing like that,' he said. 'That's just stories to keep children inside at night.'

'Not even soldiers went out after dark,' Lulianne said, 'and skulls were found, human skulls. People were murdered.'

'Not by Clan, we don't kill people.'

'You keep saying Clan, but what is it?'

'After the Contaminations, after the Fatters came out of Glass and they and their slaves killed thousands of people so rivers of blood flowed through Tip, a mob of people got together. They met in secret. They met in shadows.' Egan paused for effect, the way Aunty Bree always did when she told this story. 'They were days when no one could be trusted. Fathers informed on their children, children informed on their mothers. Anyone could be Security. Anyone could be a Glass agent. This mob decided that a life ruled by fear, secrecy and murder was no life. They were mostly young, back then, and as strong as they could be. They were the free thinkers, the visionaries. They saw past Tip and into the mountains and decided to risk everything for a small piece of real life.'

'Oh boy,' Gran said, 'you tell it the slow way. Lass, a group of them walked away from Tip. It was a small group, no matter what Egan here says, a hundred or so. Some didn't make it, of course. We watched them go — our loved ones among them. I was a girl, then. Can remember this boy trying to tell me to go with him, begging me. He was eaten by a big cat on the way, never made it to the mountain.'

'So there are really people living up there?'

'Sure are,' Egan said, 'and living well.'

49

'So if you live so well up there,' the girl said, winding her dreads around her fingers as she spoke, 'how come you're here then? How come you're back in Tip?'

'I come here regularly,' Egan said. 'I pick stuff up at Casino Market, do a bit of barter, catch up on the news. We came from here, North Tip, most of us. And one day, the Aunties reckon, this will all be Clan. We'll all live like Clan.'

'And just how do they expect that to happen?' Lulianne said.

'They hope,' Amos's quiet voice sliced in. 'They hope that one day Glass will destroy itself and just disappear and with it the Glass way of doing things. No more dope, no more worker robots, no more Tip. Just Clan and the Aunties.' His voice was carefully flat.

'You don't think it will happen, do you?' Egan asked.

'Not by itself. Tip will have to bring down Glass. The Fatters are getting old, Security is getting soft. There's too much voddy and dope, too much carni and not enough real work. Our time's coming.'

'Shh, it's mad to be talking this way,' Gran said. 'Attend your meetings, boy, if you have to, but stay out of trouble and don't get us into any, either. We do okay. We're alive and that's a hundred percent on being dead.'

'We're dying slowly,' Amos said, 'and you think that's doing okay?'

Gran didn't respond, just clicked her tongue to the roof of her mouth and turned back to Tilley.

'She's starting to look a bit better,' she said. 'See, she's less that grey smoke colour?'

Egan looked at the battered woman. He couldn't see what Gran was seeing. She looked the same colour to him — death grey where her skin wasn't burning red or purpled and yellow from the bruises. However, the rasping breath had eased, but he hoped they weren't witnessing the calm that sometimes came before death.

'Look,' Amos said urgently, 'we're getting ready. We have to. What do you reckon is going to happen when the Fatters start to die? They're going to panic. They're going to want spare parts. They're going to want sons and daughters. They already want sons and daughters. And sometimes they get them but they're all inbred. There have been round-ups in East and South — a handful of kids. All girls. Now why do you think that would be, eh?'

There was silence. Egan felt goose pimples on the back of his neck although there wasn't even a shiver of a breeze in the close room.

'All girls,' Amos repeated, 'for the Fatters to breed with. They tried it the other way a couple of years ago, but it didn't work. The women were already too old. How would that be, eh, Egan, rounded up to sleep with someone as old as Gran. Could you do it?'

'I um, well …'

'Go on.' Gran suddenly laughed, a sound like a wild camel braying, and Egan had to jump away as she made her hands into little pinching mouths aimed at his chest. 'You'd do it for Gran, wouldn't you?'

'Leave him alone, Gran,' Lulianne said. 'Look, he's blushing!'

'You're not the man for me. Don't want a blushing fool. Save it, Egan, for some young thing, save it for the airdancer here. Or have the Aunties got someone picked out for you?'

'I'd eat him alive,' Lulianne said. 'Wouldn't I, mountain boy?'

'They're tough up in the mountains,' Amos said. 'You'd be surprised, Lulu. I wouldn't go making too many wild claims.'

'Tough,' Lulianne said, and then pinched Egan quickly on the arm, 'but good-looking!'

It was a relief when Amos got back to his hobbyhorse. 'Well, they don't make them like him in Glass,' he said. 'They're old, fat and worried.'

'Doesn't do to make trouble,' Gran insisted. 'There's no trouble from Tip, not these days.'

'There will be,' Amos said, 'there will be. We will rise up and bring that conting place down.'

'Don't use that kind of language, boy,' Gran said sharply.

'Look around you, old woman. Think a rude word less is going to make any difference to our lives?'

'Oh, you and your revolution. Come on, boy, we'd better get back to Water — got an honest living to make. She's looking a bit better, our Tilley. But there'll be more waiting yet. You, Egan, you'll be eating and sleeping with us tonight?'

'Thanks, Gran,' Egan said, 'I'll come later. Might go and ferret through a Dump first.'

The little room looked a lot larger after Gran and Amos had left. Egan felt awkward, left with Lulianne. His arm burned where she had pinched and he waited for her to say something else. But she just continued to bathe Tilley's hands and, very gingerly, her face, with the water they had collected, as though she hadn't said that he was good-looking.

'I'm not good with sick people,' she said, catching him looking at her. 'My mother was sick and I hated it. Everything I did to try and help her only made her worse. Or that's what it felt like.'

'You're doing well,' Egan said. 'You're so gentle.'

Lulianne smiled. 'Thanks,' she said.

'That Amos,' Egan said. 'He gets worse and worse.'

'He's got together a kids' army. They train and stuff. I don't pay too much attention. I just want to do my job, keep things simple, stay out of trouble. I want things to be like they were, with Circus.'

'Why did you leave?'

'The Circus left. Birdie, one of our members, died.'

'That's tough,' Egan said, wanting to touch her. 'That's really tough.'

'Yeah, it was.'

Egan heard tears in her voice and reached out to pat her shoulder. 'You're doing well,' he said, and was surprised when she turned away from him abruptly. 'That's not an insult,' he said to her back.

There was something about her. It felt good to just sit by her. She might be a bit quick to take offence but she was cheeky too, flirty, and Egan wanted to show her that he could be, too, with a bit more warning. Well, maybe not cheeky exactly, but a little less gawky. Still, she had said he was good-looking, and that had to count for something. Egan was smiling to himself when Amos came by later.

'You've got all the girls, Mountain Man,' Amos said. 'Here's another one wants something.' And he jerked his head towards a girl Egan knew slightly.

'Good day, Burr.'

'Hey Egan, how's it going? Listen,' she said without giving him a chance to answer, 'there's a feral hunt on tonight. Want to come?'

'Yeah, sure, where are you hunting?'

Burr indicated the direction Egan had come from. 'They reckon there's a big one,' she said. 'Could do with a change from gruel. You should rest up, Egan. You'll need to if you're coming with us!'

* * *

Burr called for him late that night. She was already ashed up so only her eyes and teeth gleamed in her dark face. 'Here,' she said, 'get this on you,' and she wiped ash over his face. 'You look good,' she said, laughing. 'You look like one of us.'

He might look like one of the Tip children, but he found it hard keeping up with them. They ran like a pack. And then they stopped, seemingly on some unheard, unseen signal, although it wasn't clear who, if anyone, had made it or was in charge.

'Here we are,' Burr said, coming up behind him silently. 'This is where she is, the big cat. Got a cave up there in the rocks. Got kittens, too — they'll be tasty.'

'You're going after a dam?' Egan asked. 'You're all loonies. She'll fight like you've never seen!'

'Oh, we've seen it,' Burr scoffed. 'We've seen it all before, mister layaround. Them kittens are plenty tasty! But don't you feel obliged to do nothing. You're just looking here, getting some huntin' tips to take back up the mountain, eh?'

'Right,' Egan said, but he was pleased he had his good knife with him.

'Get him somewhere safe,' a small boy said to Burr. 'We don't want to have to worry about him.'

'Over there then, Egan,' Burr said. 'You'll seen it all from that bit of overhang, and we're not luring her over there.'

Egan went where he was told. It wasn't his hunt and he was lucky to have been invited to see it. He knew that and didn't want to offend anyone. Nonetheless he watched with one hand on his knife.

There was a wild howling sound, so like wild dogs that Egan started and looked around before he realised that it came from the children. They had grouped themselves in various positions around the cave entrance. A couple had shimmied up trees and sat precariously on the thin branches. One of these had a gun, Egan was surprised to see. Weapons of any sort were forbidden in Tip, but possession of firearms meant instant execution if Security discovered you with them. Perhaps Amos was right and Security was getting soft. Or were the inhabitants of Tip just more desperate?

The children kept up the howling for a while and then changed to a low growling — the kind of sound dogs made when they were protecting a kill. They growled and yapped like pups fighting over scraps. Any feral, particularly a hungry female with kittens, would be sitting in the cave thinking about the easy pickings being chewed over just outside her home. She'd have to come out and investigate.

A movement from the children was the first indication to Egan that the feral had come to the mouth of the cave. He couldn't see the big cat. He just saw that the entrance to the cave had magically cleared of children. They'd simply melted away, leaving only one — the boy, Egan thought, who had spoken to him before — hunkered down and apparently defenceless. Bait.

The cat growled. She was looking for the dogs she had heard. She was wary, but not too concerned. Egan watched as the cat, crouching down, slowly gathered herself together ready to spring. Despite everything — her thinness, her mangy fur, and even despite the danger — Egan found her beautiful. Just as she uncoiled into her leap, the boy leapt to one side, a movement that put the cat off balance. A knife aimed at the cat's neck caught her left shoulder and bounced off bone. The cat spun in the air and turned to face the children, who were now silently out in the open and holding their positions with unnatural calm. Egan saw her look back to the cave. It was too late, the way was barred by more children.

She growled menacingly, but it was obvious that the sheer number of children had confused her and she was torn between escaping and getting back to her kittens. The children, taking advantage of her hesitation, moved in. The cat turned her great head from side to side, growling. Just when it seemed to Egan that she'd made up her mind to spring for the cave, knives sliced through the air. It was risky using knives at such a distance. The children should have had arrows or spears. One of the knives made contact, though, and wounded the animal's rump. She swung around to see what it was and copped another in her neck. She was scared now and had only one instinct — to protect her kittens. The children had regrouped in perfect silence and now there were more at the cave's entrance than there had been previously. The cat didn't care, she sprang anyway, and as she did the children closest sprang too, towards her.

Egan nearly closed his eyes. He hadn't seen anything so plain suicidal in any of his Clan hunts. But even as he was starting forward, knife pulled out, he saw the big cat go down with a grunt that spewed blood on the ground. They'd got her in the belly as she sprang. By the time Egan arrived, Burr and the others were already wiping the blood from their knives.

'Gotta get the kittens, now,' Burr said cheerfully. 'Think there are three or four of them. They'll fight fierce for all they're only little. And it's dark in there. We got a torch, though. Want to come?'

'Sure,' Egan said, as steadily as he could. 'Sure I want to.'

The torch was a stick with a fuel soaked bit of felt at one end. A boy called Glue lit it and they followed warily into the cave.

'Conting hell,' Glue said. 'She's got a conting mate!'

A big cat sprang out of shadows, straight at Glue. There was a blast of gunfire as Glue went down. The cat faltered and then gave a strangled growl as it collapsed on top of the boy.

'Glue's had it,' someone shouted, 'but he got the feral. Good on Glue.'

'Come on, let's grab the kittens,' Burr said beside Egan.

They killed the kittens with grim efficiency, silenced by Glue's death. No one cried for Glue. They didn't even haul him back to Tip. A girl they called Jezz shut his eyes and straightened out the broken body.

'A hunting death, better than a Tip death, Glue. You died well. As we eat the wild, now let the wild eat you.' Everyone joined in the last part and then they made their way back to Tip.

'You'll eat with us?' Burr asked Egan as they trudged back.

'It feels wrong to just leave him there.'

'No use bringin' him back with us,' Burr said, surprised. 'What'd we do with him in Tip? Nuh. He'll be something else's meal where he is — some dogs or other ferals. Hey, who knows, Egan, next hunt we might be eating something which has eaten Glue. That'd be kind of beautiful, wouldn't it?'

Egan shuddered. 'I don't know,' he said. 'It sounds gruesome to me.'

'Oh you're soft, Egan, for all of your walking down from Clan. You're nearly as soft as a Fatter.' Then, looking up at Egan slyly, she said, 'Well, maybe not as soft as a Fatter.'

'Thank you,' Egan said, 'thanks a lot. We hunt at Clan.'

'Ya hunt with stuff, though, don't you? You hunt with rockets and nets and carry-on?'

'Sometimes, but we use knives, arrows and spears too. And you had a gun. Which you shouldn't have, you know. You could be executed for that.'

'Security don't take no notice.' Burr shrugged. 'They don't care. They're soft as you, Egan. Anyway, we have to have a gun, Amos says. We've all learnt to use it, too. We're an army, Amos says, our day will come.'

'So did Amos get you the gun?'

'I dunno who got the gun,' Burr said, 'and I wouldn't go about asking too many questions, Mister Clanman. Don't do to ask too many questions round Tip no more. Things is changing.'

'Good hunt?' Amos asked when Egan finally stumbled into the little shanty.

'A boy called Glue was killed,' Egan said. 'So no, I guess it wasn't. But it didn't put anyone off their food.'

'Who can afford that kind of luxury?' Amos asked. 'Poor Glue. He was a brave kid. One of the best. May your belly always be full, little brother, sleep well. How many cats did they get?'

'Two full size and three kittens.'

'Good protein, then. ' Amos said, and rolled over and went back to sleep.

Egan couldn't get to sleep quite so easily. He was unnerved by what he'd seen and Burr's last words kept going around and around in his head. Tip was changing, the children were wild, in a scarily controlled way, and then there was Lulianne who had shifted his universe a little to one side of centre. He wanted to see her alone, to really talk to her, find out more about her, without her stomping off. He wanted to take her somewhere private, where they could really talk. Maybe he'd sing one of the Clan songs, or play her a tune on his pipes. Soon, dreams of Lulianne put the strange night out of his head, although none of it made for easy sleep.

The Fatters imagine they can control us with dope and voddy and then stand back to watch us kill each other for the privilege. We have to recognise that dope and voddy are as lethal as the weapons Security carry. I'm not saying don't use them, but I am saying, see them for what they are and beware.

from *The Lessons of Amos from North Tip,*
Healer and Revolutionary

'Burr and them have been on a hunt,' Tick told Lulianne, 'a feral hunt. With Egan.'

'I didn't know you went hunting.' Lulianne was binding the girl's hair with strips of felt.

'We didn't always used to but Amos said we should learn, so we do. Different lots of us go on different nights. It's part of our lessons with Amos.'

'What do you hunt for?' Lulianne couldn't think of anything close to Tip worth the trouble of a hunt.

The other girl shrugged. 'Ferals mostly. Sometimes wild dog. Whatever's out there we can eat.'

'I can't imagine you hunting. What kind of weapons do you have?'

Tick shrugged, 'Just whatever.'

'Why did Egan go?' And why wasn't I invited, Lulianne wondered, but didn't say that aloud.

'Must have wanted to,' Tick said. 'Must have asked. Or maybe he likes Burr.'

'Likes Burr?' She saw Tick look at her slyly. 'Well, Burr! Prickly as her name.'

'Maybe Egan likes them tough and wild,' Tick said. 'But what's it to you if he does?'

'Nothing,' Lulianne said quickly. 'Nothing at all.'

'Go on, Gran says you pinched his bum. You must like him.'

'It was his arm, not his bum, and you shouldn't be gossiping with Gran.'

Tick rolled her eyes. 'You should ask him down to a grogger at Casino Market.'

'Haven't got enough cash, otherwise I might.'

'Ask him anyway. Egan's always got cash or something up his sleeve. Go on, Lulu, he doesn't really like Burr, I was just teasing. You must have seen the way he looked at you yesterday. Gran said he was smitten. Amos and me'll look after Ma. She's getting better. You deserve a night off.'

Lulianne thought about Egan, how he'd picked up half the bucket with her and how generously he'd given all the oil to Tilley. Lulianne would bet he'd been going to barter it down at the Market. It would be worth something, she knew that. He hadn't begrudged it for a minute, though, just handed it straight over. She remembered that even when he blushed his eyes held hers steadily. They were brown with flecks of gold in them, warm eyes.

'Yeah, you're right.'

'Hey, Lulu, finish my braids before you hare off!'

She found him cooking outside Gran's shack.

'Smells good, Mountain Man,' she said, crouching beside him. 'What's that you're putting in it?'

'Dried herbs from Clan,' Egan said, looking up and smiling at her. 'Adds a bit of something to the gruel. Want some?'

'Only if there's enough.'

'Oh, there's plenty,' he said easily.

'Did you go hunting for it last night?'

He shook his head. 'They got ferals,' he said, 'and lost Glue.'

'Glue? A wiry little redhead?'

'You got him.'

'Sleep well, little brother,' Lulianne said and drew two fingers down in the air as though she was closing his eyes.

'We say something like that in Clan,' Egan said, 'but we say "dream of us".'

'Dream of us, little brother. I don't know, maybe in Clan you're sure they'll have sweet dreams. Where I come from, sleep is more reliable.'

They sat silently for a minute, locked in their own thoughts, and then Lulianne shook herself.

'In exchange for that good-looking gruel,' she said, trying to make her voice sound careless and brash, 'I'd like to offer you a night in a grogger — voddy, music and laughs — but I don't have the cash.'

Egan laughed, 'The gruel's not that good.'

'I mean it,' Lulianne said. 'I mean, that's what I'd like to do. I'd like to take you out drinking and laughing, if you're game.' Maybe there was more gold than brown in his eyes, specks of it flickering as though the sun had caught them and set them dancing.

'I accept your generous offer,' Egan said, 'but let me pay and why don't we skip the grogger and just buy a bottle of voddy and take it up the hill somewhere? The groggers — I don't like them that much. They're such sad, desperate places, okay?'

'I haven't got my gruel yet,' Lulianne said, 'but if you like to dish up we could make it a deal.'

'It's a deal.' He handed over a plate and watched her as she took the first spoonful.

'Oh, that's good,' she said, 'that's very good. Makes your tongue jump, doesn't it? That kind of sharp, fresh taste in the pale taste of the gruel?'

'Makes your tongue jump,' Egan repeated. 'Yes, you're right. A lot of herbs do that. I suppose that's what they have to do. The gruel fills you up but the herbs give you something to wake up for. Here, Amos,' he broke off to call inside the shack, 'come and get your tongue jumping.'

Amos staggered out, patting his hair down with one hand.

'Morning. Hey, Lulianne.'

'Hey, Amos. Listen, Tick's going to help with Tilley tonight, okay?'

Amos looked between Lulianne and Egan, raising his eyebrows, 'And why would that be?'

'We're going out to have a couple of drinks,' Lulianne said. 'Egan and me. Having a night off.'

'You're welcome to come,' Egan said quickly, 'if you want to.'

'I don't drink, thanks. Got enough to do.'

'Come on, Amos,' Egan said, 'don't you need to cut loose sometimes? Come with us anyway, you don't have to drink.'

Lulianne wished he would shut up. Did he *want* Amos to come with them? Sometimes boys were so stupid. Maybe he wanted Amos along for protection!

'It's good of you to ask me,' Amos said grinning at them both, 'but I've really got things to do and I'm sure you'll have just as good time, if not better, without me.'

'If you could check Tilley ...' Lulianne said.

When she caught up with Egan late that afternoon he had on the cloak she admired and carried a light swag. He had tidied up his goatee and narrow sideburns and the rest of his face was scraped smooth. Lulianne shivered a little to imagine how sharp his hunting knife must be to get such a close shave. She felt suddenly shy and a little grubby.

'I thought we were going up the hill,' she said, 'not anywhere special.'

'Up the hill is special with you.' Egan smiled down at her. 'You always look great. I have to do some business, you know, don't want to scare the punters.'

'I'll be back,' Lulianne said.

'You watch yourself,' Gran said, peering at Lulianne as she quickly washed herself as best she could in the greasy water. 'Drink voddy and anything can happen.'

'I've drunk voddy before,' Lulianne said, wishing for once that there was some kind of screen in the room. She could feel the old woman's eyes scrutinising her naked body. 'Everyone in Circus drank it and there was never a problem. Well, not until Birdie died,' she amended, 'but that was Nemrick. Anyway, we're not just going to drink voddy. We're going to talk. Get acquainted.'

'I'm just saying watch yourself,' Gran said. 'Girls like you think you know everything, but still waters run deep and you can get hurt diving in without looking.'

Lulianne stared at the old woman. 'I don't know what you're talking about.'

She didn't feel much cleaner after her wash but at least she smelt a little less. Some of Birdie's fragrant oil would have been a good thing. Birdie had used it to sweet-talk Nemrick into anything she wanted. It was a heady smell that got stuck in your nose and could have overpowered even the stench of Tip. But on the other hand, had Egan shaved for her, or for his *punters*, whoever they were? Anway, she didn't have any of the oil. Nemrick had poured it out in a drunken fit of grief and rolled around in the perfumed ground, wailing.

Lulianne released her dreads from their topknot and let them fall around her face, framing it in a bright straggle of colour. The dye was beginning to fade, but the wild pinky orange was still more vibrant than anything else in Tip.

'Here, girl.' Gran waddled up. 'I shouldn't be encouraging you but you look so ... I dunno, just alive.' And before Lulianne knew what she was doing the old woman had reached up and dabbed behind her ears.

'Oh, Gran, I was just thinking of that smell. Birdie used to wear it. Where did you get it?

'Don't ask questions, just give us a look at you. Yeah, you'll do.'

'I can't thank you enough,' Lulianne said, her nostrils full of the heady, beautiful smell. 'I just can't.' She felt tears fill her eyes and partly it was Gran's unexpected kindness, and partly because the smell reminded her so sharply of Birdie.

'Just be careful,' Gran said. 'Oh, and have a good time, getting acquainted with the Clan boy. He's a good feller, Egan. Yeah, and you're a good girl.' The woman nodded, 'You're both family. So look after each other.'

It seemed to Lulianne that the whole Tip could smell her. Every time she shook her head, waves of the strong fragrance eddied out. Men home from the Dump watched her as she walked past. Someone whistled low and menacingly but

Lulianne paid no attention. The perfume filled her with careless joy.

'Hey, look at you,' Egan said, when she sauntered up, her eyes already bright at the thought of the night ahead. 'By contaminations, Lulianne, you look great and you smell ... what is that?'

'Something Gran put on me. Birdie used to wear it, too. Come on, Egan, let's go, eh?'

They walked down to Casino together. On either side of the path open trenches took the Tip effluent down to a water-reclaiming dam. Lulianne was used to the stench and paid it no attention, but Egan wrinkled his nose in disgust.

'I don't know how the Fatters can live with this on their doorstep,' he said, waving his hand in the direction of the monolithic glass structure. 'It's disgusting. It really is.'

'It's just Tip,' Lulianne said defensively. 'I bet you have things up where you live that smell just as bad.'

She was surprised when the young man beside her laughed and took her hand. 'Come on, I'm not having a go. I'm just saying if I was Inside, I'd be thinking about how to get rid of it — not just doing the odd round-up here and there.'

They continued to walk hand in hand. As they got closer to Casino, street sellers stopped them, peddling everything from bits of mechanical refuse to dope. Lulianne watched as Egan scanned the stalls.

'Can't take most of this stuff,' he said regretfully, fingering some old bits of filter and pumps. 'Too hard to carry back. Shame. Mind you, there's good scavenging back home. Ah, there's Stretch, he's my man. Come on.'

They approached a gaunt figure who didn't even have a

makeshift counter or trestle, just a few old cooking utensils laid out on a rug in front of him.

'What are you getting from him?' Lulianne whispered.

'Cash,' Egan said. 'I've got some stuff for him. What you see with Stretch isn't what you get. Understand?'

'Sure.'

'Ah, Egan.' Stretch turned in their direction and Lulianne saw that he had the Milk Eye and was nearly, if not entirely, blind. 'A friend with you?'

'The airdancer,' Egan replied. The two men did not embrace but touched their palms together, the traders' sign of fellowship.

'Heard of her. Quite a spectacle, they tell me. Smells like she scrubs up well.'

'Thanks,' Lulianne said. 'I am here, you know.'

'Sarky bitch, eh? So what, Egan? You doing business or out on the lair?'

'Business first,' Egan said.

'In front of the tart?'

'She's safe,' Egan said. 'She's been looking after Tilley's kids.'

'Yeah? Heard about that. Bad business. All right, what you got for me?'

Egan unpacked some things carefully from his pack. Lulianne didn't want to appear too curious, so she stood back, but even from where she stood she could see the odd collection of phials and bottles Egan produced. While the transaction appeared like any other street sale, Lulianne noticed that both men were quietly hurried and that Egan used his body to block off any passing interest. To the casual observer, these were two men squatting and gossiping, maybe haggling over the price of a dented pan. The bottles were passed between them swiftly and all the while Stretch kept up a loud running commentary on the state of Tip. Only Lulianne's sharp eyes saw Egan tucking a wad of cash in the pouch he wore inside his shirt at the conclusion of their business.

'We're out of here. Good to see you, Stretch.' The men touched palms again and then Egan rose in a graceful movement and he and Lulianne set out for the groggers.

'Voddy, eh?' Egan said. 'Where do you reckon?'

Lulianne surveyed the Casino scene. The groggers were as close to the low ornate building as Security would allow them. Each tent was surrounded by dull-eyed, largely silent drinkers. They were mainly worker robots on their way home from their shift or on the way from their shift to the casino. They were drinking courage or remorse or just addiction. There were no street performers here, no drummers, as there would have been in Defence. Instead Security patrolled everywhere, their white shirts startling in the grey crowd. At the doors of the casino Security checked ID cards and anyone who handed over a suspect one was immediately hauled off into a barred vehicle. Lulianne shivered and walked closer to Egan.

'Everywhere is much the same.'

Egan looked down and smiled at her. 'Come with me. Stretch recommended a place.'

They pushed their way to a crowded counter and a large woman looked them up and down.

'Stretch sent us,' Egan said, 'for a bottle of your best.'

'Show us the colour, then,' the woman said, leaning forward so that her massive breasts rested on the counter.

Egan pulled out a note, seemingly from his sleeve, and laid it between them on the counter.

'Looks good,' she said and the note disappeared quickly between her breasts. 'Here you are then, mister. Watch it, it's good strong stuff.'

Egan pocketed the bottle and they headed up past a Casino, past Tip and on, steering clear of Main and heading into the low-lying scrub north of Tip. It wasn't long before they were well away from the noise and smell of Tip and out into mound country. The sun was setting in a lurid wash of colour in the west.

'Do you mind being out here?' Egan asked.

Lulianne shook her head. 'Walked through here with Adri, when I left Circus Despoir,' she said. 'This country doesn't bother me.' Though I miss Adri, she thought to herself. She'd left the big dog back with Tilley and the children. She hoped no wild dog packs were roaming around.

'I don't mind this country,' Egan said, 'but home's not so scrubby. We've got some real trees up there. And the Auntie's reckon that they could have here, too, if the Fatters stopped poisoning everything. The Aunties reckon they do it as another way of keeping everyone in control. You can't plant in ground so poor and constantly poisoned. I can't understand why everyone keeps living here when they could just get up and go, go to Clan where its clean and things grow.'

'It's this stuff, isn't it,' Lulianne waved the voddy bottle at him, 'don't you reckon?'

'Not for people like Gran, Tilley and Amos, it isn't.'

'But anyway, it might be clean and whatever, but aren't the Aunties just like Glass anyway, keeping everyone in control?'

'No. It's not like that at all. Here, you going to drink some of that, or are you just holding on to it?'

Lulianne took a swig. It was like clear fire. Unlike most of the voddy she'd tried, there was no aftertaste of slightly rotting matter.

'You must have paid top cash for this,' she said, passing the bottle back to Egan.

He shrugged. 'Tasting different voddys,' he said, ' to compare with back at Clan. Trying to get the perfect combo. It's harder than you think. One lot exploded.'

Lulianne laughed. The moon had come up and she could see Egan's face. The moonlight softened its sharp planes, making him look as gentle as she knew he was.

'People just like being where they know,' she said. 'Like, what's back at Defence for me, eh? Nothing. My mum's dead, has been for years. Circus isn't around. Wouldn't go back if it was. There's nothing there. Nothing. But I keep telling myself I'll get back to Defence. I tell stories about it all the time — how they dye stuff for you at the market, dip it in these huge vats and pull it out different colours. How little girls make some kind of living just braiding hair all day. How the street girls call to the soldiers. I dream of it, too. It's just home. Like Clan is for you and Tip is for Tillie and her kids and Gran. People don't like leaving home, whatever it is. They're scared. You and I, we're lucky. We go different places. That is lucky, I reckon.'

'I used to think so,' Egan said, 'now I don't know. I just think there are more places I want to be, more people it hurts to leave.'

'Hey, don't go getting sad on me, Mountain Boy. Here,

70

have a drink. Tell me, what was the hunt like? Was it exciting?'

She watched him swallowing a mouthful of voddy.

'Was until they lost Glue,' he said.

'Hey, come on Egan, play your pipes. Don't get gloomy.'

'I'm not. I'm just thinking. What kind of tune do you want?'

'Something light, something you can move to.'

'You going to dance?'

'I'll see how I feel when the music starts. See you play. If it moves me, I just might.'

He pulled the pipes from his pack and blew a couple of preliminary notes. 'I can't always tell what will happen, what'll come out,' he said, 'it's like the pipes tell me sometimes, not the other way round. I know that sounds stupid, but it's just how it is.'

Lulianne moved closer. 'It doesn't sound stupid,' she said reaching out and putting her hand on his leg, 'it sounds right. It sounds how music should be. You just play Egan, I'll listen to anything.' She left her hand on his leg. The first notes wavered a little, as though they were uncomfortably aware of her listening. They jumped around, not settling into anything, sweet sounds but just sounds, nothing you could put together. She cosied up closer to Egan and he paused from blowing to let her settle against him, then he resumed playing and it started happening, the notes began to form patterns, like groups of stars, in the sky. They lilted and looped, dancing together with a soft, plaintive undertone sounding a small, almost unheard warning that everything was fleeting.

'That was beautiful,' Lulianne said when the music died away. 'Just beautiful.'

'It's how you make me feel,' Egan said slowly. 'That's what the pipes told me. And here's something else, I think. Something maybe you can dance to.'

This tune was different — wilder, the notes chasing each other up and down. Lulianne couldn't help it, she was on her feet in a minute, clapping time and stamping out the beat. The music got faster and dust rose from underneath her stomping and her skirt flew out and blurred into a moonlit whirl of colour. Just when she thought she'd collapse, the music slowed down again. A little bridge of notes sounded between the fast bit and the next which was gentler, almost wistful, and Lulianne swayed in time, until in a small flourish, the tune ended.

'You're a great player,' she said flopping down next to him and grabbing the voddy bottle. 'That was just terrific, Egan. Thank you.'

Egan took a swig and handed the bottle back to her. 'That was you,' he said, 'that was Airdancer's tune.'

'What's your tune, then?'

'I don't. I don't know that you can play your own? What do you think?'

'If you can't, who can?'

'Well, I just wonder — I might want to put too much into my own song, you know? Whereas I'm happy to just play the bit of you I see — and maybe hint at something else, but not try to get everything. I reckon if I tried to play me, I'd try to put everything in and it would all be muddled and busy and no one thing would come through strongly enough to pull it all together.'

'I reckon you think too much, Mister Mountain Man. But I reckon you're okay.' Lulianne leaned against him again, nudging his arm up so she nestled underneath it. Egan put the pipes away and then put his arm around her.

'It's lovely out here, isn't it?' she said after a bit. It wasn't that the silence bothered her, it was just that she wanted to retain the connection with Egan, to be sharing something still.

'It's quiet,' Egan said, 'and it's better than Tip, but it's not lovely, exactly.'

'You're supposed to say anywhere with me is lovely,' Lulianne laughed. 'Don't you know the rules, Mountain Boy?'

'I was just going to say that I'd sit with you in the moonlight anywhere — in the middle of Casino — and your presence alone would sweeten the air and lighten the world.'

'Hey, that was a lovely thing to say. You can kiss me now if you want.' Lulianne lifted her face up to his.

'I mean it, Lulu. That's what you do, you make everything sweet and light.'

'And I meant that you could kiss me,' Lulianne said, leaning towards him a little. 'Or don't you want to?'

'Oh, I want to all right.' Egan said.

'But the Aunties wouldn't be happy?'

'The Aunties haven't anything to do with it.' Egan said, but he still didn't kiss her.

'I'm getting bored,' Lulianne said, but she still waited.

'You're really important,' Egan said, his arm tightening. 'I don't want this to be just tonight, because of the voddy or the music or the moonlight.'

'We haven't had that much voddy,' Lulianne said, 'or *I* haven't. I can't speak for you.'

'The thing is,' Egan said, 'I belong in Clan.'

'So?'

'Well, you keep talking about going back to Defence.'

'What I said was I kept talking about it. I didn't say I was going. I said we were lucky that we traveled to different places. We can live anywhere.'

'It's beautiful up at Clan,' Egan said, 'but you feel some-times that there's no world, you know? You feel as though all there is in the world is you and Clan and the trees you see every day and the wild dogs howling at night. You forget about Tip and Glass. You're just watering the garden, hoping things will grow. You hope there's enough food to feed everyone this season. The Aunties are there talking, talking, always talking about Clan. Always what's best for Clan.'

'See, it's not all there is, is it?' Lulianne said, jabbing at the ground with a bit of rock. 'Nothing's all anywhere. I don't think it ever was. I think you always want something differ-ent.' She wasn't sure what she meant. 'So I suppose you can kiss me, then. If you want to.'

Egan bent down to her and their mouths met. They kissed for a long time, slowly at first, as though learning the shape of each other's smile, and then more urgently until their breath was fast. She broke away from him, to calm her heart down.

'Better than voddy, eh?' she said when she could trust her-self to speak.

He laughed, a glad sound in the night. 'You're telling me,' he said.

'I like your laugh. It sounds as though the whole world's happy.'

'You make my world happy.'

She leant forward and kissed him again. It was good to be here with Egan, knowing that he liked her as much as she liked him. Nothing else mattered.

'I really like you, Mountain Boy,' she said, and traced his mouth with her finger. 'You're smiling.'

'I like you, Airdancer. I really like you. Would you come to Clan with me, meet the Aunties?'

'Yeah, I might, if you ask me nicely.'

'Come back with me when I go?'

'Maybe.'

Egan's chest was broad. Lulianne lay her head against it and listened to his heart beating. Above them the stars whirled and danced. She reached up to stroke Egan's face and he kissed her fingers.

'Look at the stars,' she whispered, 'Egan, look, they're spinning just for us.'

At the heart of Clan are its children. If you learn nothing else, learn to enter a child's time. That will tell you all you need to know.

Auntie Teece, Clan

Egan woke with a start. One arm was around Lulianne. With the other he was holding down a great dog's head against his chest. A wave of dog sweat and musky odour almost choked him.

'Get out of here,' he said, shoving at the dog in panic. Was it part of a pack of wild yellow dogs? Where were its pack mates? But the dog whined suddenly and pushed Egan's hand away to lick at Lulianne's face. It was her brindle bitch, Adri.

'Adri,' Egan hissed and could hear the dog's tail thump on the dust. 'What are you doing here?'

The dog whined again and pushed Lulianne's head with her long, sensitive nose.

'She's asleep.' Egan yawned. 'It's not even full light, Adri. What do you want?'

Whatever it was, the dog wasn't taking no for an answer. She gave Egan a cursory lick on his face and padded around to the other side of the makeshift swag. Egan watched the dog, confused. All he could really think about was the sweet weight of Lulianne on his shoulder. He stroked her pink dreads with his hand. She didn't stir. In sleep she looked like a child, all the sun-lines and living erased from her face. Egan let his fingers stray over that face and in her sleep Lulianne smiled.

The brindle bitch looked at Egan and growled, not exactly

·threateningly, more in a *pay attention to me* way. And then she nudged Lulianne again, quite hard, in the side of the girl's neck. Lulianne stirred. The dog pushed again, making a throaty noise as she did so. Lulianne moved away from the wet nose and snuggled further into Egan's arm. The dog barked, sharply, right in Lulianne's ear. Egan jumped. The noise was explosive. Lulianne started awake.

'Adri?' she said. 'What do you want? What are you doing here? You're supposed to be with Tilley and the kids.'

Adri barked again.

'Adri, shush, it's too early in the morning. Be quiet. Leave us alone.'

Egan pulled her back to him. 'We smell like each other,' he said sniffing.

'It's my perfume,' she said, 'it's good isn't it? Hey, Mountain Boy, you smell as good as I do.'

The dog whined and pawed the ground.

'Do you think she wants something?' Egan said finally.

'Must do. Good to wake up with you, Egan.'

'Good to wake up with you, Airdancer. This could be addictive.'

'Shall we begin where we left off?'

'Here do you mean?' Egan started to kiss her, starting with her eyelids.

Adri barked again.

'Go away with it,' Lulianne said. 'I wonder if she's jealous?'

'Come here, Adri,' Egan said and tried to rub behind the dog's ears but she pranced away from him and just stood there, half whining, half growling.

'She's never done this before,' Lulianne said sitting up.

'Not that she's had reason to, either. I don't normally spend my nights kissing ... Oh no, look Egan, her leg!'

Egan leaned over. 'Contaminations! Oh god, Lulianne. We've got to do something about that.' The dog's left hind leg was laid open to the bone. 'No wonder she wanted to find you.'

'Here girl,' Lulianne said gently. 'Adri, here.' The dog whined and put her head on Lulianne's lap. 'I'll have to get her to Amos. He'll know what to do. Dogs aren't that different to people. I mean, their wounds aren't, are they? Oh, Egan, how do you think she did it?'

'I don't know,' Egan said. 'I can't see how it could have happened. Unless someone ...'

'She was with Tilley and Tilley's kids. They wouldn't hurt her.'

'Of course *they* wouldn't, but maybe someone else did?'

'We'll have to go back.'

'Yeah, we will. But I reckon we should do what we can for her here. Look, we could pull that skin together, I think. I've got a healing oil here — not as strong as the one we used with Tilley, but not bad, either.' He squatted down beside the dog, pulled out a small leather pouch from inside his shirt and took out a small phial. 'Do you want to put it on her?'

Lulianne shook her head. 'I'll hold her,' she offered, 'if you put it on?'

'Do you think she'll mind me doing it?' He eyed the dog warily. Adri was a good bitch but her teeth were as sharp as his hunting knife and he didn't want to offend her.

'She'll be fine, but can you do it?'

'Of course I can.' He'd bound up his own dogs many times before but suddenly, in front of Lulianne he felt clumsy, as though his fingers were bigger than normal. He took a couple of slow breaths to calm down and looked steadily at the wound. It didn't look great. Flies were already gathered on it, and he had to wave them off before sprinkling the precious oil into the wound.

'What are we going to bind it with,' he said.

'Move, girl,' Lulianne, shifted the dog's head from her lap, stood up and took her skirt off. 'Got a knife?' she asked.

He handed over his hunting knife. 'Careful, it's sharp.'

She sliced off a wide band of felt and then pulled the skirt back on quickly.

'That's a good length,' Egan said, smiling at her. 'Lulu, I'll be as gentle as I can be but I think it will hurt her. That's bone there.'

Lulianne shuddered. 'Don't tell me,' she said, 'just do it quickly.' She sat down again and took the dog back on her lap, holding her firmly but talking too, all the time in a low lilting voice.

'We're going up to Clan, girl, the Mountain Boy and you and me. He's taking us to visit the Aunties, isn't that right Egan, so the Aunties can see us. We're all going to Clan away from Tip. Going to see some trees, rather than this scrub. Right, Egan?'

'Right,' he replied mechanically, his fingers busy. 'And Adri's going to chase paccas. Aren't you girl. Chase paccas and take down a feral. You'll be right, girl.'

Together they talked to the dog as Egan bound the wound with felt, patiently pulling the jagged bits of skin together as best he could.

'Done,' he said finally and they both exhaled in one

breath 'It'll be all right until Amos can do a better job. She's tough, Lulianne, she'll make it. Look at her.'

The dog had scrambled to her feet and was wagging her tail. She licked Egan's hand, as though to thank him.

'Good girl,' he said. 'Good dog, Adri.'

'Thank you,' Lulianne said. 'I know that oil stuff is worth a bit. Thanks for using it on her.'

Egan shrugged. 'It's okay,' he said. 'There's more where that came from, back at Clan. We'd better get a move on, don't you think?'

'Yes, but first,' and she held out her hand. Egan took it and let her draw him close. For a minute they stood like that, then he bent and kissed her quickly. 'One for the road.'

'Wish we could just stay here,' she said, 'but we've got to get her to Amos.'

'It's okay.' Egan felt uneasy, too, although the dog had probably wandered out of Tilley's shack and got on the wrong side of some aggro drunk. That was all. Nasty, but probably nothing the dog hadn't seen before.

When they got in clear sight of Tip, they both stopped dead and stared. There were people everywhere, it seemed, in clusters and groups, but no normal Tip activity.

'Something has happened,' Egan said, nudging Lulianne forward. 'Look!'

Lulianne squinted against the harsh morning light. 'Come on Egan, quickly!'

They broke into a run, the dog loping beside them. A little closer and they could hear a strange wailing.

'Can you hear that?' Egan asked. 'Is it ... '

'It's the Mourning,' Lulianne said urgently. 'What's happened? Who's dead?'

Egan grabbed her hand. 'Run,' he said urgently

They arrived panting at Water, where the people were congregated listening to Amos, who was speaking from the low wall. 'We must rally, friends,' he said. 'It is time. The Fatters have taken our future. What are we going to do about it? Wail or act?'

'What happened?' Lulianne interrupted, running up. 'What's happened, Amos?'

Amos crouched down to speak to her and Egan directly. 'The bastards took the kids. They just came in the middle of the night and grabbed them. It was planned and quick. Just hauled them off. Some didn't even wake up, I reckon. But some did — a mother was bashed to death as she tried to stop them. Before anyone really knew, they'd piled them into these vehicles and taken off with them. It was dark. No one could see anything. There was just a lot of confusion, yelling and shots.' His words were jerked out as though each one was painful to utter.

'Tilley's kids too? Not Lovie? Not Ned and Tick?'

'Everyone,' Amos said. 'Even Tilley's kids.'

'We'll have to get them back,' Lulianne said sitting back on her haunches.

'Right,' Egan said, hoping he sounded as fierce and determined as she did.

'We'll get them out,' Amos said. 'This is it, isn't it, comrades? This is it.'

Lulianne and Egan looked at the small crowd in front of them.

'Burn Glass to the ground,' a man in front shouted.

'Yeah, burn it down.'

'That won't help the kids,' Amos said, 'that'll just get them killed. We need to get the kids out before we do anything like that.'

'Glass is impenetrable,' Egan said. 'You need an ID card to get through the main gates. If you don't have an ID card, you're shot. It's that simple.'

'There's got to be ways in,' Lulianne said. 'There's simply got to be. You can get in anywhere, if you just know how. There'll be a weakness, for sure. There always is.' She sounded more confident than she felt.

'Through the roof, maybe,' Amos said. 'They've got all the hydro labs up the top. But you'd have to be a bird to get in that way. You'd have to fly.'

'Well, that's it then,' Lulianne said. 'Looks like I'm going through the top.'

The two young men looked at her, speechless.

'I practically fly,' she said. 'I'm an airdancer, after all. I just need some wings.'

A long silence greeted her words.

'No, I should do it,' Egan said finally.

'You can't, you're too heavy,' Lulianne said. 'And anyway, you don't have that kind of experience. And Amos can't. His medical skills will be needed. No, Egan, it obviously has to be me. It makes sense.'

'Won't they be expecting an attack? Won't Security be doubled?' Egan asked desperately. He couldn't bear the thought of Lulianne, all by herself, going into Glass. It was unthinkable.

Amos snorted. 'They won't bother doing that. They'll go back to their dope and their voddy without bothering to look under the surface. They never do. They're stupid and soft, the Fatters. And Security isn't much better. Cowards. Just conting cowards.'

'She can't go in by herself,' Egan said, 'she'll be killed.'

'She won't be by herself,' a woman said, 'we'll all be behind her. Amos will make sure of that.'

'Yeah, of course we will,' a man joined her. 'We'll be there. We'll do anything.'

*   *   *

'We'll have to find out as much as we can about Glass,' Egan said. 'There must be someone in Tip who knows. Someone with information?'

'There's a good informant, a worker robots who Tilley shacked up with for a while,' Amos said slowly. 'He's a tough, close bastard. We'll need to bribe him. He wouldn't give out anything for nothing.'

'I've got some cash.' It was Gran's voice. Everyone jumped. 'Didn't think I was around, eh?' she said. 'Gran's everywhere. She hears everything. I think it's the daftest plan I've heard, mind. Plain stupid. Going in the top. Never heard anything like it, but I can see by the set of her face she's going to try it. Daft girl. Better not send her with the money. You boy, you go. Amos will tell you who to look for. Can't spare Amos. There's a couple of shot wounds, a few beatings. Doubt they'll live, but you never know.'

Egan wondered, not for the first time, whether he really liked Gran. Yet he respected her tireless work for Tilley and he knew she had standing in Tip. He found her manner off-putting, though, and her toughness — real or not — disconcerting.

'I'll willingly go,' he said, straightening his shoulders. 'Just give me the cash and tell me who I'm looking for.'

Egan bailed up his contact between the great doors of Glass and the Casino. He was easier to pick than Egan expected, a big fellow, whose very walk suggested a belligerence exacerbated by dope rather than subdued by it, as was normally the case. His size must have made him too useful for Security to get rid of him — troublemakers were usually dispatched quickly. Egan, dressed in the same grey uniform as the worker robots, fell in to step beside the man.

'Going gambling?' he asked casually.

'What's it to you?' the man asked, not even bothering to look at who addressed him.

'I might have something for you that'll change your night's luck,' Egan said, striding out a little to keep in step with the man.

'What are you talking about?'

'In exchange for information,' Egan said, 'let's call it a gift, from one punter to another.'

The man looked at Egan for the first time and Egan looked right back, although he winced inwardly at the man's misshapen face. His nose was knocked sideways, one of his eyes was glassy with White Eye and his mouth looked as though one side of it had split at some stage and been sewn roughly back with a blunt needle. Egan didn't let his gaze falter.

'Meet you round South side of Casino,' the man said finally. 'There's a grog shop there. I'll have a double voddy.'

'I'll be there,' Egan said.

He found the bar without any trouble. It was a quiet bar, populated only by men and one working girl, too out of it on dope and voddy to be trying terribly hard. As Egan walked over to the bar, she wolf-whistled and gestured suggestively, but when he didn't respond she just took another swig of the voddy in her glass and continued to hum tunelessly.

Egan bought the man's voddy and carefully chose a squat near the edge of the activity and waited.

'So what do you want to know?' The man downed half his drink in one swallow.

'Heard you might tell us about Inside, for a payment.' Egan's voice was low but he didn't bother to look around to see if they'd been overheard. He didn't want this bloke thinking he was scared.

'Cash?' the bloke asked, downing the drink and holding out his glass for Egan to buy another.

'You give us the info, we've got the cash.'

'Make it another double,' the man said, 'and I'll see what I can do.'

When Egan came back there was a rough map drawn on the dirty table.

'You're after the kids,' the man stated.

'Yeah, we're after the kids.'

'Don't know why you bother.'

Egan shrugged. 'That's for us to worry about.'

'Here we are then,' the man said. 'Ground floor is storerooms, general stuff, some Security quarters, though most of them live over with the worker robots in Rail. This is the second storey — that's where the Fatters live. Third's labs — carniculture, medlabs, their experiments — and the fourth's the hydro labs and some recreational units, because of the light, see?'

'And the kids?' Egan asked.

'We haven't seen them. They've had Div 5 working on them. You know what Div 5 is?'

Egan shook his head.

'They're the workers nearest Disposal,' the man said without a flicker of pity. 'They're the oldies. They've got them cleaning the kids up, in case of contagion.' He shook his head disinterestedly. 'Don't want anything to spread to us useful ones. Do you see?'

'What do you do Inside?' Egan asked.

'Hurl stuff around,' the man said in a flat voice. 'In other words, none of your business.'

'Fair enough. Do you know where the kids are being kept?'

'They've quarantined them in a disused section of the top floor. Less likely for anything to spread from up there, and some stupid theory about the sun killing off some of the diseases. It's way down on the East block.'

'Heavy Security up there?'

The man snorted. 'As if. They're getting soft up in Glass. Not like the old days. They'll force dope into the kids. Keep 'em quiet. They do everything with dope now. Half of Security is permanently skittled. They've got the usual — two guys patrolling the floor with semis — but the kids will be zonked out, won't cause any trouble. And the Fatters know you lot aren't going to be able to do anything. They won't think you'd bother risking your lives for a bunch of lousy kids.'

'Never had kids yourself, then?' Egan asked as casually as he could.

'Wouldn't know,' the man said, finishing his drink and looking at Egan calmly. 'Wouldn't know and wouldn't care. Take it from me, boy, shit happens out here, all sorts of it.

And then they dispose of you. The only things worth keeping on for are voddy and the machines. That's it, boy. That's this life.'

'Any way into Glass?' Egan asked.

'Not conting likely, unless you've got wings and plan to fly in.'

'Wouldn't know what they're planning to do with the kids?'

'I've heard the rumours,' the man said, 'that say the children are an army. Ha! Bunch of louse and disease-ridden bandies like that an army! What some people can let themselves think! Still, I heard they killed a man who tried to mess with the Airdancer, so you never know. Heard the doctor boy teaches them. Amos. Hear his name a lot. But I'd say it's more likely they're keeping 'em for spare parts. The Fatters are wearing out, you see. They've lived a long time but they're on their last legs. And there's no live births in there. More kids are born in Tip. Makes you wonder, doesn't it? Maybe you need a bit of dirt and grime just to keep going, eh? Yeah, word is they want to live forever, the Fatters, and they'll make more of themselves, just like they make carni.'

'That's not right,'

The man shrugged. 'Give us your cash now, boy. I've got luck to attend to.'

'Well, thanks,' Egan said, shaking his hand formally and passing the cash at the same time.

The man walked straight out and disappeared towards the Casino. Egan studied the dirt map for a while. His informant had been surprisingly thorough, even though the drawing was rough. He'd concentrated on the hydro lab area but had marked in all the entrances and exits and indicated the routes of the great staircases and conveyors that Egan had heard joined the various levels and snaked throughout the whole city. He'd marked the section the kids were in as well, and he'd even indicated which of the great roof panels could be opened. He may have been belligerent and uncommunicative, but his information was worth every bit of the cash Egan had handed over. Punters often had strange moral tics, Egan thought, wiping the table clean. They'd beat up a fortune-teller, they'd cheat the machines, if they could, but they had a strange respect for anyone betting against the system.

And that's what Lulianne was doing, Egan thought, trudging back to Tip. That's what they were all doing. What had possessed them, thinking they could do that? Nonetheless Egan felt more alive than he'd felt even tilling the ground up in Clan. It was the idea of doing something for once against them. Even if we fail, Egan thought, even if we're all killed, we will have tried to do something. Something unimaginable. Something big.

Kids were killing themselves, that's why the children's army started. They'd look around them, see their future, and they'd blow their brains out with a stolen gun or overdose on stolen dope and voddy. They had nothing that belonged to them and they belonged to nothing. It was okay for those with families — like Tilley's kids — but a lot of them were strays or had folks who were slowly killing themselves on dope and voddy. The army wasn't a game. It was a way of belonging, of caring and of hoping.

from *The Lessons of Amos from North Tip,*
Healer and Revolutionary

After they'd watched Egan set off, Lulianne and Amos went to check on Tilley. She was certainly much improved but that just made the whole thing sadder. Tilley was getting better, but her children weren't there to see it.

'It'll have to work,' Lulianne said fiercely to Amos as he checked Adri's wound. 'I can't bear the thought of Tilley asking for her kids and we have to tell her, oh guess what, they're trapped in Glass — that is, if they're not already chopped up. I just can't bear it.'

'Adri will be okay,' Amos said. 'Did you and Egan have a nice night?'

'Yes, we did.'

'He's a good bloke, Egan,' Amos said.

'He is,' Lulianne said.

From where they were sitting the ritual wailing of the women floated up in waves of sound. It was an unearthly sound. Lulianne shuddered.

'You okay about going in?' Amos asked.

'I would hate myself if I didn't,' Lulianne answered. 'If we can find a way to get in through the top, I'm going.'

They sat in silence for a while, the women's wailing the only sound around them.

'I like you,' Lulianne said suddenly, reaching for Amos's hand. 'I just want you to know that. You've been a really good friend to me here.'

'I like you, too,' Amos said. 'You are a good friend, too. And I think you and Egan look good together.'

He stroked her fingers lightly. He had longer fingers than hers, but their palms were the same size, although hers were calloused from using the ropes and the harness. Amos's hands were soft in comparison and very clean.

'Yeah,' Lulianne said, 'we do look good together. Oh Amos, why does everything have to happen now?'

'Everything happens when it happens. There isn't a good or bad time. Now, our beliefs and our hope, are all we have.'

Lulianne went back into Tilley's shack. The air in there had cleared. The sick woman was cool to her touch and, for the first time, seemed to be asleep rather than unconscious or delirious. Lulianne dragged her sleeping mat out and lay down on it. Before she had even called Adri, the great dog was at her side and settled down, too, with a sigh. Lulianne knew she should be thinking about the mission at hand, the kids locked in the city, Egan doing deals, but she couldn't focus on anything. She just felt numb and very, very tired. She hugged Adri to her.

Lulianne thought about Lovie, remembering her small hands against her own, but she couldn't cry about it. Everything, even Egan, or maybe especially Egan, seemed very far away and the only thing that was real was this tiredness weighing down her eyelids. Lulianne gave into it, shut her eyes and slept.

She woke to feel a hand stroking her hair. When she opened her eyes, she saw Egan sitting cross-legged beside her, Adri's head in his lap.

'Didn't mean to wake you,' he said.

'Oh yeah?' Lulianne couldn't help grinning at the lie.

'Well, maybe. I gave the dog some pacca jerky and she ate it all and I've got news. I've got lots of news. Where's Amos?'

'Gone to look after people.'

'Okay. I'm going to find him. In a minute.'

He leant down and kissed her lightly. The crazy wailing, the knowledge that there were women dying in Tip, the thought of the children locked up in the city — all that useless tragedy faded from Lulianne's mind as she pulled Egan down to join her on the sleeping mat.

'If anything happens to me in Glass, Egan, I want you to take Adri, okay? I know she'll be safe with you.'

'I don't want to think about that,' Egan said, tightening his arms around Lulianne. 'I don't want to think about that.'

She felt his kisses on her head and reached out to stroke his face. She could barely see him in the dim light of Tilley's shack but she realised with a sense of shock that she knew the expression he had on his face anyway.

'But you'll take her?' she persisted. 'She trusts you, Egan. She let you bind her leg. She wouldn't let everyone do that, you know. And you gave her the pacca and not everyone would have done *that* either, not just for a dog. Please say you'll take her. She's not much of a hunter but she gets the occasional kill. You could train her, I bet. You could.'

'She doesn't have to hunt.' Egan's words were buried

91

somewhere in Lulianne's dreads. 'Of course I'd take her. But nothing will happen. You're going to go in and out of Glass and nothing's going to happen. You're not going to let anything happen, Lulu. I've got plans. I've got plans for us. And I think I even know how you can get in. Come on, we'd better find Amos. The sooner we get this sorted the better.'

They met Amos, who looked exhausted.

'Give me a couple of minutes,' he said, 'and I'll go clean up in Water and meet you by the old pump.' There was blood on his clothes and on the dim oil lamp lighting his three patients.

When he met them at the pump, he'd washed out his shirt, which was already drying in the sticky heat. 'Well, you're here to catch me up with further developments?'

'Yes, the man was very useful indeed.' And with speed and efficiency Egan recreated his informant's map of Glass in the sand at their feet.

'So you'd go in through the hydro labs?' Amos asked.

'Right over the top,' Egan said. 'See Lulu — these panels slide back, for air and cleaning. They'd be closed at night, of course. You'd need some kind of lever probably to jimmy them open. The main problem is getting up to the roof. And that's where they think they've got it beat. No outside pipes, gutters, nothing you can get purchase on. The roof's the only part that isn't sealed as tight as a disposal bag. There is an emergency exit, several, in fact, but they're tunnelled under Tip, and this bloke reckons half of them have caved in and the other half are toxic. Anyway, they'd only land you bang smack in the middle of Level One.'

'But how is she going to get in over the top?' Amos asked.

'Yeah. Well, that's the tricky bit,' Egan said, 'but I reckon it'll have to be rockets.

'Rockets?' Lulianne said, and Amos echoed her.

'Yeah, I've been thinking. We do it up at Clan sometimes, when we need to. Launch a net at a herd of paccas with rockets. Then we pick out a few old ones to kill for winter hides. I don't see why we couldn't do the same thing here. The beauty of it is that I don't need much. I've got the makings with me, practically. I'd need a good length of pipe, something to make a kind of fin with — but it should be pretty easy to pick up that kind of stuff. Lulianne needs gear to climb with and some kind of grappling hook.'

'I've got hooks in my kit,' Lulianne said. 'I need rope, that's what I need.'

'It'd be good to get something lighter than rope, if we could,' Egan said.

'So what does the rocket do?' Amos asked.

'Launches the rope and the hook up to the roof of Glass. At the very least there'll be a water drain rim or something for the hook to catch on to. Your man said the whole roof is sliding windows, so there'll be a latch, something.'

'There always is,' Lulianne said. 'That's the joy of the hooks — you can use them practically anywhere. There used to be this building in Defence that was supposed to be completely sealed. They'd built it in the old days, sealed the top brass in, and it was supposed to be impossible to get up the walls. The walls were made of this pressed kind of metal — like mirrors — and they'd heat up. People reckoned you could cook carni on them — if you could get the carni. Anway, Birdie climbed up them. She performed from the roof for a bet. It was a lot of cash. The hook had attached itself to something up there. Later she told us it was just this tiny lifted corner, nearly rusted through. A wonder she didn't fall that day, but she didn't. That was some act!'

'Well this isn't,' Egan said sternly, 'it's a rescue mission.'

'It's sounding a bit looney,' Amos said. 'Rockets, hooks — you think it will work?'

'It has to. Look, Amos, I reckon Tip could get organized to burst into Glass — people are upset enough, but that's not going to help the kids. People will get hurt, badly hurt. Security will just kill and kill — it will give them the excuse they want. I go in, I go in quietly, I get the kids quietly and then we think. At least the kids are out. We could — I don't know, get them up to Clan, maybe, Egan?'

'That would be the best idea,' Egan said.

'They won't go,' Amos said, 'they're an army. They'll want to stay where the action is.'

'Well, at least they'll be Outside.' Lulianne turned away from the two men. Inside she could feel a buzz of excitement. It would be a great act. The greatest. She felt the same way she'd felt whenever Birdie suggested a new twist to their act. She smiled at the city in the distance. I'm going in there, she thought, I'm flying in.

Egan broke into her thoughts. 'I'm going to have to go back, down to Casino, for some cable, if we can get it. The powder I have isn't enough to launch a huge length of rope. I want something lighter, if possible. And some rocket-making stuff. And I'll need more to barter with. It could be expensive, what I need.'

'I'll see to that side of it,' Amos said straightening up, 'if you really think this will work. I'll see you get what you need. And maybe more. When do you need it?'

'Well, I could go down again tonight. They'd have a change of Security, wouldn't they? That might even be better than waiting. But only if you can get the cash.'

'I'll start now, and we'll see how I go.' Amos said and limped off.

'What do you think he's going to do?' Egan asked Lulianne.

'He'll do what he has to do. Amos always does. No matter what. He's quite ... hard, really. It doesn't show through much, but he is. He'd loot bodies if he had to. He'd do it.' She wondered how she suddenly knew that, and looking up at Egan's face she knew that he recognised the truth of what she had said as well. She slipped her arm through Egan's. 'Honestly, if anyone can organise Tip, it's Amos. You're really going to go down tonight, to Casino?'

'Yeah. I need to get started as soon as I can. I don't think those kids have much time. But we have some time, now, don't we? That we could spend together?'

'I'd like that,' Lulianne said. 'I'd like that a lot.'

People don't leave Clan. Why would you live anywhere else? If you left it, you'd miss everything — the people, the talk, the gardens. You'd be orphaned from your whole life. It would be the worst thing in the world.

Aunty Teece, Clan

Casino Market at night was as busy as it was in the daytime. Many of the vendors camped where their stalls were, always open for business. Some were dozing, others were zonked on dope. Quite a lot of dope was changing hands, Egan noticed. A group of musicians had set themselves up near one of the grog shops and a small crowd of people swayed and danced to the music, passing a bottle of voddy between them. For a moment he wished he had encouraged Lulianne to come with him. She would have enjoyed the music. But she'd been exhausted. Tilley had woken and she'd had to explain to Tilley what had happened, keeping the story as mercifully short and hopeful as possible. Tilley had raged and wept, but she was still so weak from her injuries and infection that she had quickly tired herself out and drifted back into a fitful sleep.

Egan wasn't particularly happy with the rescue plan but he had to concede that it was the only one that had any chance of success. It would simply have to work if they were all to survive. He rubbed the charm he wore on a string around his neck. It *must* work. It would be too much to bear if anything happened to Lulianne. They'd only just found each other. They hadn't had enough time together.

Amos had given him the name and whereabouts of another man. He wouldn't need cash, it was all set. The man was safe and had the kind of stuff that was needed. Since the

96

children had been rounded up, Amos moved through Tip grimly but with an edgy efficiency.

Egan picked up his pace and headed into Casino Market. It didn't do to think about the future. You did one thing at a time, took one step after another, and then everything that had to happen, would. That was what the Aunties said, and they were right. If you spent all your time worrying you'd be burnt out before you started and that wasn't useful.

It didn't take Egan long to find his man. He had the brightest felt shelter and some night-lights. He had connections. The two men nodded at each other and Egan explained quickly what he wanted. The other man listened attentively.

'Doin' some climbing, then?' he asked.

'Could say that.' Egan was noncommital.

'Sounds mighty like it. I could have exactly what you need. Got it in Defence. They use it for routine training exercises. Or did. When the boys trained. Good stock. I've got other stuff you could use, if it's climbing you're doing.'

'It is climbing,' Egan admitted reluctantly.

'Got some gloves, then. You'll need gloves. Got some useful belts, too. You'd want to put together a bit of a kit, wouldn't you? For when you're up whatever it is you want to get up? Like, you'll need a weapon, I'd say. To get you out of trouble. You might need a bolt cutter, even. Climbing's like that, isn't it? Full of nasty surprises. I've got a set of security passes — you know, the ID cards. These are usefully blank. You imprint your fingerprint on 'em. Of course, you've got to get inside before you can use them, but once you're inside they'll open a few doors. Or did, last time I had reason to lend 'em out.'

'Amos told you?'

'I got the general idea. Anyway, unless you're planning to go mountain climbing' — the man waved his hand nonchalantly in the direction of Egan's mountains — 'there's only one place you'd want to climb into, isn't there? Stands to reason.'

'True enough. Keep it quiet though, the less people ...'

The man gave a short laugh. 'Let's just say that Amos says things to the people round here who can make things happen. It's not all as hopeless as it looks. Amos is moving, boyo, and we're all part of it, in our own ways. Behind the talk, people are doing things. People are gettin' ready. It's not all weeping and wailing and carrying on like a bunch of ghost people. There are strong people in Tip, strong and determined. You do your bit and see who's behind you. Here, I've got your kit together. Tell that Airdancer of yours the gloves'll be on the big side and she'd better see that you rope 'em on her securely. She won't want her hands shredded.'

Egan found himself walking back to Tip with a bag of stuff he hadn't even looked at.

He unpacked the bag on the floor of Tilley's shack. 'Contaminations,' he said, 'look at this, Lulu. Look at this cable, it's just perfect — light and strong. You'll shimmy up this, girl. Providing the grapples hold. Providing it all works. And here, he's given you a pack. It's ex-Defence. Look, state-of-the-art stuff, Lulu.' He sat back on his heels.

'This is fantastic,' Lulianne said, 'must have cost a fortune.'

'Cost nothing. He gave it to me. Can you believe it?'

'That was amazingly generous. There must be a year's cash in this.'

'More, I reckon. How did he get it?'

'Don't ask. I never do.' Amos said from the doorway. He nodded at them both and limped in.

'This is what we've all been waiting for. Something bigger than any of us, something that'll galvanise Tip, make 'em act. We've got the numbers, we can do it.'

'It's dangerous.' Egan said.

'It's worth it, Egan. It's time. There's always one action that tips the balance, one new oppression people can't live with. This is it. The Fatters have done it this time. Think of what's in Glass. Everything we need. If we had what's in Glass, we'd change Tip forever. We'd thrive, not subsist. Even stopping their damned poisoning would change our lives, just that one thing. Why do they do it? Just to keep us powerless, so we're dependant on their Dumps. Imagine being able to grow our own food here in Tip. Imagine that.'

'I know,' Egan said, 'it could look like Clan.'

'It could be Clan,' Amos said, 'instead of Tip. Clan with more technology and better medicine. Five star Clan.'

Egan laughed, 'I like it,' he said, 'Five star Clan. You wouldn't get the Aunties to agree.'

'Now listen, you two, we're planning a distraction to cover you going in. It'll get Security's attention and leave the way clear for you.'

'That's a good idea,' Lulianne said, 'anything to cover the sound of Egan's rockets.'

'It is a good idea, if it doesn't get out of hand, Amos. Do you think you can keep it under control?'

'It's the best idea I've had,' Amos said. 'Can you think of anything else?'

'Not really,' Egan admitted reluctantly. 'It just worries me.'

'It worries me, too,' Amos said. 'We don't want anything going off at the wrong time, but we need something — those rockets of yours are hardly silent. If we're got some kind of rowdy protest going on, it'll get them right away from where you'll be. With any kind of luck you'll get a clear go.'

'We need that,' Lulianne said.

She was right. They needed everything they could get in their favour. The equipment was fantastic, but they still had to use it. Egan put his arm around Lulianne and hugged her close.

'We've had good luck so far getting the information, for a start, and now all this gear. If our luck holds, we'll be fine.' He wanted to sound optimistic but felt he'd overdone it.

Lulianne rubbed her head affectionately against his chest. 'We'll do it.'

Sometimes you just happen to be in the right place at a time when history is being made, but that doesn't mean anything by itself. Anyone can be in that place and turn their back on it. You have to be prepared to act. That's the difference. We were prepared.

from *The Words of Amos from North Tip,*
Healer and Revolutionary

Lulianne lay as close to Egan as she could and traced her fingers lightly over his back.

'Are you awake?' she whispered.

'Yeah,' Egan said, and rolled over towards her. 'Can't sleep.'

'Neither can I. Want to talk?'

'What do you want to talk about?'

'I dunno. Anything except tomorrow.'

'I'll miss you, when you're inside,' Egan told her, and she could feel his fingers tighten in her dreads. He was holding on to them as though he could anchor her to the ground. In a strange way Lulianne was looking forward to climbing up that thin cable. It was the gig of a lifetime even though no one except Egan would see her. She'd know she'd done it and it would be something she'd never forget — if she lived to remember it. She'd be the Airdancer who flew inside Glass. She liked it.

'I'll miss you,' she told him. 'I'll think of you.'

'You go with my love,' he said. 'You know that, don't you?'

'I know that, Egan.'

'You've been happy here, haven't you? Teaching the kids?'

'Yeah,' Lulianne admitted slowly, 'you're right. I've been happy here. I guess it is the kids. Was the kids.' She changed the subject. 'Tell me more about the garden. Come on, Egan, tell me about a Clan day. Start from when you get up in the morning.'

She listened as Egan described his day, utterly caught up in the little details he sketched for her.

'The morning's the best time,' he said. 'I like to get out when the sun's only just up. Then the world feels new and the garden's all fresh. Everything is dewy, Lulu. The sky is just light, sometimes you can still see the moon and you fill your lungs with all the clean air. You own the world then.'

'Tell me about the others at Clan. Who are your best friends? Who have you been in love with?' It was like being a child again, like she had been with Birdie, begging her to tell about when Birdie had joined Circus. It didn't matter what they talked about. They were just like little kids too scared of the dark to sleep, telling each other stories to see them through the night.

Egan told her about the boys he'd built the voddy still with and how they'd got drunk on voddy, much to the Aunties' disgust.

'What about love?' Lulianne teased him. 'You haven't mentioned that.'

'I haven't been in love before,' Egan said, holding her more tightly. 'Not like this. Not the way I feel about you. What about you? Who have you been in love with?'

'No one.' Lulianne felt shy. 'No one at all. All I did was Circus. I was happy, just doing Circus.'

'We feel right, don't we?'

'I know you,' Lulianne said, 'as though you've always been part of my future. I feel as though I had to meet you.'

'I walked into Tip and there you were — I watched, you know. I saw you fall from the Tower. You were like flower petals. I never saw anything so beautiful.'

'That's the Airdancer, though, that's not Lulianne.'

'But I fell in love with Lulianne later. When you were so snipey carrying the water bucket.'

'I was worried about Tilley,'

'I knew that.'

'So do you have fun at Clan?' Lulianne wanted to break the silence that had descended like a sudden cloud.

'We have good times, ' Egan said. 'It's all simpler — there's nothing sinister. No one out to get you, except maybe the odd feral and sometimes packs of wild dogs, but they're only trying to feed themselves and their young. It's straightforward, you know, not messy.'

'I like Tip, though, the messiness. Well, some of it.'

'I know,' Egan hugged her. 'I do, too. Sometimes.'

'I wish it was over. I wish it was all over and you and I were on the Soltram, heading north to Clan.'

'We have only to get through tomorrow. First thing we'll go up somewhere in the hills, warm up, practise and then this time tomorrow night you'll be Inside. We'll get through it, Lulianne.'

'Play something, Egan, play us a getting through tune.'

Even in the dark she could feel how he unwrapped the little bone pipes from their felted bag with care. She loved how he handled everything — the calm precision he brought to each task, whatever it was. Now, he blew softly, testing each true note before stringing them together in a simple, sad little song which wound around her like smoke.

She didn't know how long he played. The tune seemed to go on and on, rambling through her dreams as she lay in the safety of Egan's arms, his heartbeat sure and steady, a low drum underwriting the melancholy pipes. This is all we have, it seemed to say to her, this breath and the next, nothing else is as certain as this. In her dreams she walked with Egan but she wasn't ever sure where they were and the landscape changed randomly. At one stage they walked through skeletons and the shock of the trees turning from branch to bone jerked her back into the real night. Egan was still playing and she drifted off again, back into their journey but this time the trees remained trees and grew thicker, wilder and more green than anything before in her life.

When she woke properly, Egan was still curled around one side of her while Adri stretched along the other. She could see sunlight and hear someone moving around the inside of the shack.

She stretched carefully, rolled Adri out of the way and padded softly into the back of the shack. Tilley was up and shuffling around, lighting the little burner in one corner.

'Tilley!'

'Shh, you'll wake him,' Tilley said, bent over the burner, not looking up.

'You shouldn't be up.' Lulianne crouched beside her and blew on the little flame until all the burners were alight.

'Thanks, Lulu. No, well maybe I shouldn't, but I'm not going to keep lying in bed as if I'm dying, not when there's so much happening. Think I'm going to miss it all? Thought I'd have today as a kind of practice day. You know?'

'That's what we're going to do,' Lulianne admitted. 'Here Tilley, I can fix that, you sit down. If you do too much today you'll flake out tomorrow.'

'True.' Tilley sat back down on her sleeping mat. Lulianne felt rather than saw the older woman's stiffness.

'So how do you feel?' she asked, in her best cheerful voice.

'How do you reckon?' Tilley asked sharply. 'Kids rounded up, face beaten up, one eye practically bung. Oh, I feel like a picnic. Is that what you wanted to hear?'

Lulianne didn't look up. She measured out the tea, trying to keep her hands steady. She was close to tears suddenly. It had been a stupid question. There was only one answer. Tilley was right.

'I'm sorry,' Tilley said later, holding the flask of tea carefully between her trembling hands. 'You didn't deserve that. You've been fantastic, Lulu and I should be thanking you, not shouting at you. I am so sorry. Can you forgive me?'

'It's okay,' Lulianne said. 'No one's in a good state today.'

'Amos was pretty cheerful when he came in earlier,' Tilley said. 'He was positively gleaming.'

'Yeah, well, Amos was probably just pleased to see that you've come through his rough doctoring! You're his miracle.'

'It's a bit more than that,' Tilley said. 'He's been planning what to do while you go in over the top. He's wired, that boy.'

'I'm just concentrating on what I have to do,' Lulianne said.

'Good idea. You and Egan had better both have some good nourishing gruel,' Tilley said. 'There's some dried meat and meal there. I'll make it.'

'I'll do it,' Lulianne said. 'You just rest, Tilley.'

She soaked the meat in the water left over from the tea and emptied the meal on top of it, ignoring the mealy bugs that also fell in. She stirred slowly. It was just a busking gig, she thought, as she stirred, that was the way to deal with it. Ignore the knots looping in her stomach and the cramp in her bowels. Just a busking gig, she repeated to herself and tried to empty her mind of everything but the smell of the gruel rising in the foetid air of the small shack.

'Smells good,' Egan said, emerging from the other room. 'Oh, Tilley, you're up and about.'

'Don't want to miss anything,' Tilley said gruffly. 'Not with you two doing your bit.'

'We'll get them. Lulu will get them.' Egan laid his hand gently on Tilley's shoulder. The gesture was what Tilley needed, Lulianne realised, seeing the woman look up at Egan. Why hadn't she been able to do that? She saw Egan walking around his garden, laying his hands on the plants, the plants rubbing against his touch like great green animals and smiled, feeling better. They could do it. Together they could do anything.

The buoyant feeling lasted well into the day. After the gruel, she and Egan headed up to the hills, loaded under backpacks filled with the necessary gear. Every hundred or so metres Egan would pause and survey the land behind them but nothing so much as stirred there. Nonetheless, they didn't take a straight track but zigzagged, doubled back, always watching and listening, followed closely by Adri, still wearing her dressing.

'This will do,' Egan said eventually. They were pretty close to where they had spent the night. Lulianne recognised a small clump of melaleuca in an odd half-circle formation. Egan headed to this clump.

Lulianne knelt on the ground to empty her pack. 'Come on, Egan, let's get started.'

He pulled a small plastic container out of his pack and some light metal sheets. Next he pulled a small pouch from a side pocket and laid it carefully on the ground some way away from everything else. 'Have you got the hook and the cable?' he asked.

'Here it is.'

'Okay,' Egan said, 'what we're going to do is to make a rocket. The idea is pretty basic. The rocket goes in one direction and the hook and cable go in the other. It's rough and ready but it's all we've got.'

'What do you put in it?' Lulianne asked.

'Oh, a mixture of stuff,' Egan said. 'Rocket powder we call it. We pack it in here' — he indicated the hollow of the cylinder — 'and then we light this bit of rope and the thing will whoosh up to where the powder is.'

'So what, it explodes?'

'Sort of. Propels, actually — burns up the oxygen in the air, so forces the rocket forward.'

'Couldn't it just go off in your pocket?'

Egan shrugged. 'You've got to treat it respectfully. Now, Lulu, concentrate, because this is where you'll have to help. We'll have to attach the cable to the rocket. I'm just using this one for practice. The other one for tonight has a good ridge where the cable will loop. We'll just do the best we can here.' He fiddled with the thin end of the cable and soon had it looped around the bottle neck. 'Then we'll tuck this sheeting over it,' he said, 'and just push it into a cone shape. That'll help cut down air resistance.'

Lulianne watched his large hands working. She felt useless. His fingers seemed to know just what to do. Her time would come, she reminded herself. No one else in Tip could climb that cable. She was the only one.

'Now,' Egan said, 'I'll pack the rocket.' He took the whole thing over to the powder pouch and delicately packed a small internal cavity in the bottle. 'Don't stand too close,' he warned Lulianne. 'We can't afford an accident at this stage.'

Lulianne couldn't see how the dull grey powder was capable of doing anything. It looked just like fine gravel.

'Okay, this is the fuse,' Egan said, inserting a small length of rope into the bottle and securing it in place with a kind of plastic plug. 'Now you have to lay out the cable, Lulu. No tangles, okay — we won't get a second chance with this. It's got to go smoothly and the hook has to sail true. So that's your job, right?'

'Right.' Lulianne could feel jitters in her stomach. Just a busking gig, she reminded herself, just a busking gig. No different from equipment checks with Birdie. No different.

'All right,' Egan said looking critically at her looped cable. 'Now, you have to come in with me, holding that — you're in front, right. See that boulder there? Let's do it a hundred metres to the side of that. We're running, right? But running slowly.'

It took Egan less time to dig the rocket in than it did Lulianne to pull the cable taut, but the set-up looked okay when they'd finished.

'Right, Lulu, you get out now — scarper. I'm lighting the

fuse. So run in front but away from the hook. We don't want you grappled!'

She lingered long enough to see the brief flare and the flame whisk up the fuse rope and then Egan was beside her, grabbing her hand and pulling her along. 'Down,' he shouted and pulled her to the ground. There was a small whooshing sound and Lulianne saw the bottle rocket sail up into the air and arc over, and then she heard the whirring sound as the cable followed, the hook flashing dangerously on the end.

'Egan!' she shouted, 'look — it's gone right over the tree! It's going to work!'

Egan stood up, hands on his hips. 'Looks good,' he said. 'I reckon you're going into Glass, girl!'

'I am going in,' she said. 'I am.' She hugged him, holding him tightly.

The rest of the afternoon was spent testing the cable. It was different from the ropes she was used to working with. The tensions were different and the lack of flexibility confused her at first. It didn't feel alive under her hands the way rope did. Even though the cable itself was lighter, it felt heavier and less responsive and it took her a while to get a feel for it, but eventually she could haul herself up quite quickly, both hand over hand with the gloves and using the foot loops.

'Not elegant,' she said, 'but it will do.'

'May not be elegant to you,' Egan said, 'but it looks pretty good from the ground. You look like some kind of bright climbing bird, Lulu.'

The sun was going down by the time they got back to Glass. It was almost too beautiful to bear, a splash of bright orange which bounced off the sides of Glass and lit up the dusty piles of rubble around Tip, making them golden for a moment or two. Egan took her hand and they stood together until it disappeared and the light in the sky paled to lemon.

'It won't be long now until it's dark,' Egan said, and Lulianne heard the tension in his voice. She wound her fingers through his.

'It will be okay,' she said, glad her voice sounded sure and steady.

His fingers gripped hers more tightly. 'I've never met anyone like you, Lulianne,' he said. 'I love you.'

'I love you, too,' she said, and knew it was true.

'Come on,' he said, 'let's get this over and done with.'

Amos met them in Tip. Tilley had been right, he was glittery. He looked as though he hadn't slept for nights and his face was all sharp angles.

'You'll be fine,' he said. 'We're creating a distraction for you at the market. It'll tie up Security without costing us anything. You go up and over on the west corner. No one will hear anything from Outside. Okay?'

It was just a matter of waiting now, the hardest part. She and Egan couldn't even go anywhere private. They sat together outside Tilley's. Lulianne had changed into the drabbest clothes she owned and tied her dreads up in an old grey rag. Egan mixed up some more rocket powder and fiddled with the rocket shell he'd made. Every so often he jumped up and wandered off, looking towards the west as if trying to gauge just how dark it was.

Lulianne was glad that Adri stayed with her. She petted the dog's ears and tried to focus on making her mind as empty as the night sky. It didn't work. Instead, Lovie's face came into her mind and she found herself going over the children whose names and faces she knew, counting them and hoping they were all alive.

Tilley made them eat something but she didn't fuss. There was an unnerving quietness everywhere, Lulianne thought, as though all of Tip was holding its breath. And yet in other ways Tip was quite normal. People still walked down to Casino and Casino Market in small groups, some women hoping to trade sex for some gambling chips or grog, some men hoping to get to the dump first or to trade whatever filled their packs.

A fellow stopped close by them and seemed about to say something but instead just half-raised his arm in a kind of salute.

'One of Amos's mob,' Egan muttered, staring straight ahead. He had stopped fidgeting and sat as still as she did. She longed to be lying somewhere with him, her head on his chest listening to his regular heartbeat. Instead she put her arm round his shoulders and nestled close. His fingers stroking her neck were soothing but she could tell from the tension in his muscles that he was thinking ahead, as she was. The night grew darker and, like an echo, Glass dimmed as the great city settled into sleep.

Amos limped up, paler now than he had ever been. 'Okay,' he said, 'it's time. Ash yourselves up with this.' He handed them a container of damp ash and mud.

Lulianne dipped her fingers in and scooped up the smelly grey mixture. She painted Egan's face grey as once she had painted Birdie's with sparkling colour, making sure she worked methodically from his hairline down to his chin and then down his long neck. Then it was her turn. When he had finished he kissed her mouth, the only part of her face not camouflaged.

'You are beautiful,' he whispered.

'So are you,' she whispered back.

'Come on,' Amos said, 'you've got to go. I can't tell how much time you'll have, just that we're hoping it will be long enough. Good luck.'

Egan led the way to the west corner, ducking and weaving back on his tracks. He had a curious stooped run which Lulianne imitated, dodging as he did from cover to cover, shadow to shadow, getting closer to Glass than they had ever been. They were almost at the west corner of Glass when they heard muffled drum beats and Egan whispered, 'It's started! Amos has started.'

Lulianne laid out the cable, secured it as Egan had shown her and then ran, still half doubled over, to a nearby rubble mound. She felt Egan stumble down beside her and they both watched warily as the little flame licked up the fuse rope and there was a whoosh before the rocket shot off and then arced over. She only breathed again when they heard the sharp clank as the hook landed.

Egan gave her the thumbs-up sign and for the first time since that afternoon he smiled briefly. Hand in hand they ran over to the side of the building. It took them a while to find the fine cable, which had blended into the dark polished surface.

Egan tested it first, yanking with all his weight. It was very quiet. The only thing Lulianne could hear was the sound of their breathing and Egan's grunts as he pulled hard, swinging on the cable.

'I reckon it's caught something,' he said finally. 'It doesn't give under me.' He'd legged up a little of the cable to test it. 'I could go in, Lulu. I could probably do it.'

'No, you couldn't,' she said, 'not all that way, with no experience. Halfway up you'd start to slide back, Egan, or you'd end up pulling the hook out. You're not light or nimble enough. Here, tie the gloves on, please.'

When the gloves were in place, Egan took off the charm he always wore.

'For you,' he said, ignoring Lulianne's protests and slipping it over her head.

'Egan, you can't give that away,' Lulianne protested.

'You need it,' he said it, 'and I need you to have it.'

They stood close together for a brief second and then Egan stepped away. Lulianne took a deep breath and began to climb the cable. It was further than she had ever climbed before and she was careful to pace herself and take it gently. The dark sides of Glass gave nothing away and she was terrified that someone inside might see her, might be watching her slow progress up the cable. She prayed that the hook would hold, all of her alert for any shift, any telltale slack in the cable on which she swung like a human spider.

She hoped Egan had left and wasn't still there watching her, but she couldn't look down. All her energy was needed to keep going up. It wasn't just muscular strength or agility but something more — willpower. Any noise she made reverberated through the western side of Glass like a great bell ringing. Even with soft feral-skin shoes every time she kicked away from the side of the building she held her breath, waiting for a shout from Security or a just a shot, taking her down.

It took forever to get to where the side wall met the roof at the top. She was covered in a thin slick of sweat and every nerve seemed closer to her skin. This was when the hook was tested to the maximum, this swing from the cable to the roof guttering. *Help me.* She sent the thought starwards, as though Birdie or someone might be listening up there. The guttering groaned, bent under her and there was a rasping sound of metal tearing. A shockwave of adrenalin pumped through her. Was it giving away? She was so close too. Her mind shut down, she couldn't think of anything. She just hung on the cable, waiting for the metal to pull loose and drop her, like a stone, to the ground.

The rasping stopped, the cable held and Lulianne breathed again, slowly. There was a chance it would go but there was an almost equal chance it was okay. She gripped the cable with her feet for extra purchase and pulled herself on to the rooftop.

It was a flat roof that stretched forever. From where she crouched the great sliding panels that opened into the hydro labs were clearly visible. She took her bearings then looked down. It was shadowy and dark. She couldn't see Egan but she could feel him out there, watching her. She raised her fist in the air in a victory salute and smiled down at him, wherever he was in the darkness.

Push people to the edge and sometimes they go over, but sometimes they learn to fly. That's how we got Clan. We were pushed too far, we jumped, we flew. There was nowhere else to go.

Aunty Teece, Clan

At the last storey, he lost her. The night darkened or maybe she was just too far away to see clearly. There'd be a noise if she fell, so he stayed where he was, waiting. Only when she appeared on the roof, a dark shape framed against the lighter sky and then her fist silhouetted in a wave, did he realize he'd been clenching his teeth until his jaw ached.

He and Adri melted back into Tip, following the shadows. Tip was deserted, but he could hear a steady, growing noise coming from Casino Market and hurried down. Everyone was congregated there, filling the space between Glass and the adjacent Casino. Market stall holders edged back, protecting their goods from careless feet. Egan had never seen so many people at once.

The drummers had attracted them. There was a whole group — just drums, no other instruments. They were made from large industrial bins, some with feral skins stretched over the opening, others with some kind of pressed metal or even, plastic. People beat them with padded drumsticks or slapped them with gloved palms, casting strange shadows in the eerie gas flares which lit up the market. The beat was kept and subtly changed by the leader, a wiry man with over-developed shoulders who used both a pair of short thick drumsticks he spun so fast they blurred in the air, and his own hands. He wore a coloured headband tied around his forehead to stop the sweat dripping down his face — all the drummers did. Where had they got those from? The bands were rust-coloured, like old blood, and gave them a slightly sinister appearance.

People stood in front of them, watching and listening. Some danced in time to the beat, a hypnotic whirling and stomping dance, falling in and out of loose groups or by themselves, caught up completely in the primal sound.

Beyond all of that was a huge bonfire ready to light and in the middle of the planks and scavenged wood, was a huge effigy, as tall as two men and dressed like a Fatter. His mouth gaped in a bright rush of red right across the lower part of his face. Where was all this colour coming from? Shoved in the smeared, open mouth emerged the unmistakable figure of a child. Lifelike feet and legs dangled out as though the Fatter had bitten the child's head off. It was crude but Egan shuddered with horror when he saw it.

There was a strange electricity in the air. Egan didn't have to push his way through the crowd. People just parted to let him through and grinned at him and the dog by his side. A man he didn't know bent down to pat Adri. He wasn't at all sure that he wanted to be there, but just as the crowd had opened to let him in, they now closed around him and he could only move forward, towards the dancers, the drummers and the effigy.

'This is wild,' a woman said to him, 'don't you think? Can you feel the power?'

Egan, taller than many of the others crowding around him, stood on his tiptoes and peered through. Where was Security? They ringed the edges of the crowd, standing with their backs to Casino and Glass motionless, legs apart, hands gripping their weapons. They looked straight ahead, not at the effigy, not at the drummers or the dancers but straight back at the crowd.

Where was Amos?

'Have you seen the doctor?' Egan asked anyone he bumped into, 'Have you seen Amos?'

'He's here,' people told him. 'He's everywhere.'

Everyone had seen him, but no one knew where he was.

Finally he ran into a woman wearing one of the blood-coloured bands around her arm.

'He's over in the tents,' she said, 'where the others are. Who are you? I'll tell him you're coming. Oh, wait a minute, you're the gardener aren't you? The tall gardener. He'll be pleased to see you.'

As she spoke she brought some kind of device out from a pouch she wore around her waist.

'Sparrer to command, Sparrer to command. Gardener coming over for the doctor.'

'Where did you get that?'

'Neat, aren't they? An old batch. They use em for everything Inside. Wait till we get our hands on what they've got. We'll all live like Fatters. Imagine making all of Tip into a garden, eh? How would you like to see that happen? I've heard they've got plants in there so green they hurt your eyes. Do you believe it?'

'Yes,' Egan said. 'Yes, I believe it.'

'They're going to be ours. We're going to get them out of there, just like your airdancer's getting the kids out and we're planting a new life, a new world for us all.'

'I have to find Amos.'

'You go over to the tents. Stay safe. We'll need gardeners!'

Egan's progress over to the tents was slow. People kept stopping him, wanting to talk.

'Can't believe they're just standing there, eh?' one bloke said to him, jerking his head toward Security.

'Good likeness, isn't it? You know it's the General!'

It was hard to gauge the crowd's mood. Sometimes it felt like a party, a party presided over by the grotesque figure and his awful appetite. People were referring to the figure as the General, in almost affectionate tones. It felt like nothing Egan had experienced, except maybe, the afternoon before the three-day initiation hunt at Clan. But even that was different as some of it was spent in solitary meditation, a ritual giving up of childish things to assume the burdens of young adulthood.

Eventually he reached the tents where he found Amos surrounded by a small mob, all wearing those bands.

'Hey Egan, how did it go?'

'She's up.'

'Good work, man. Good work. Here, put one of these on.'

Egan held out his arm for Amos to tie a band around it, above his elbow.

'One of us, brother,' Amos said grinning at him. 'How does it feel?'

Egan shrugged uncomfortably. 'I don't know.'

'Do you like it?' Amos motioned in the General's direction.

'It's creepy.'

'It's real. That's what they'll do. Everyone needs to know that.'

'Oh, I think you've got the message across. What happens now?'

'We're waiting for Cruz to slow down his drumming. I'm going to get up, talk to everyone and then we'll light it up. That'll cause some mayhem.' Amos said with satisfaction. 'You wait and see what we've got planned.'

Egan felt the skin at the back of his neck crawl. It wasn't what Amos said, but the way he said it, with a kind of cheerful nonchalance that belied the outrageous caricature, the weapons Security carried and the patient tension of the crowd. How did Amos, such a slight figure, hope to contain all this?

'Do you know what you're doing?'

'Oh yes, we reckon we've got a fair idea,' Amos answered. 'What about you, Egan? Do you know what you're doing?'

'No,' Egan said honestly. 'I just lit a rocket and watched Lulu climb up Glass. I don't know what I'm doing here.'

'You're going to build a new Glass,' Amos held Egan's shoulders, 'that's why you're here. Your destiny collided with history. We need you to spread the new seeds, to show us how to raise a garden from this ash. It's nearly time. Listen.'

Egan could hear the drummers slowing down imperceptibly. The walkie talkie crackled in Amos' hand.

'Casino's cleared, except for a couple of losers. What'll we do?'

'We want everyone out,' Amos said. 'Give them an incentive.'

'Right ho. We'll start a game. Need a bit of extra time, though.'

'It's okay, Cruz has hit a groove. He's not doing anything fast.'

'What are you doing? Why do you want to clear out the Casino? Amos, what's going on?'

Amos punched Egan's arm lightly. 'I promised a distraction, didn't I? You wait. It'll distract them all right!'

The crowd seemed to settle into more orderly bunches, most of them with an arm-banded official standing close by, not obviously in charge, but there, mingling, talking and standing with everyone else. Waiting.

The walkie-talkie crackled into life again.

'You're on count down, we're all out.'

'Okay,' Amos said. 'Thanks, friend. Well, this is, Egan. Wish me luck.'

'Good luck,' Egan without thinking about it, embraced him as a fellow clansman. 'Stay safe,' he said, and watched as Amos limped forward to the platform near the bonfire. He was flanked by some of his mob, all wearing armbands. The drumming slowed to a stop and then Cruz, watching Amos approach, did an extravagant drum roll while Amos mounted the stage.

The crowd roared as Amos limped forward, megaphone in hand. Egan anxiously eyed Security as well as Amos's progress to the front of the stage. Security made no move to intercede.

Amos stood for a moment acknowledging the crowd's applause, his hands, palms outward towards them, a gesture that included everyone in his own tribute. Then he silenced them, holding his hands up.

'Thank you,' he said. 'Thank you friends. Most of you know I am Amos, barefoot doctor of North Tip, dedicated to the healing of bodies.'

He was such a frail, solitary figure on the stage. He had no weapons and no protection but his voice didn't falter as he addressed the crowd. Egan crossed his chest with his arm, a Clan gesture of protection — the Aunties did it for hunters. 'My heart is still for you, brother,' he mouthed the ritual words.

'We all know why we're here,' Amos continued. 'We're here because of that.' He turned and gestured to the figure towering behind him. 'That's what has happened in our world and we're angry. Right?'

'Right,' the crowd roared back.

Egan watched Security. They stood still and easy in their white uniforms. Around them the gas flares sputtered and gusted and the lights from Casino flared. It looked to Egan as though more Security had arrived. He felt edgy, the way he did before a hunt. He wanted to keep his eyes everywhere — on Security, on Amos and on the crowd.

'Our children are our only resources,' Amos said, calmly. 'They were all we had. We sleep on dirt, we eat it and breathe it, we live in dirt and we die in it. Why?'

'Because they want everything themselves,' someone shouted up.

'That's right.' Amos bent down, as though talking directly to the person who had answered his question. 'You're right. They want everything themselves and they're prepared to kill and poison our land, even our children, so they can go on living in that, that monstrosity. We've stood back. We've watched our friends killed. We've watched our water poisoned. We've watched our bush shrivel and die. Are we going to watch our kids feed their hunger for power as well?'

Egan lost track of time listening to Amos. There was no anger in his voice, but deep regret. He wasn't urging anyone to action, he was simply explaining why it was their only choice. The crowd was nodding, people were quietly agreeing. There was a deceptive quietness over the whole scene. It lulled Security, Egan could see that. Their formation was less severe now. They lounged, moving closer together to chat. Their hands strayed from their weapons to scratch persistent itches. Some put their weapons down on the ground and stretched cramped muscles. A couple surreptitiously swigged from a voddy bottle and passed it along to their neighbours.

They weren't listening. If they had been, they would have heard the sting in Amos's words, the patient hatred. They weren't watching or they would have seen all the weapons everyone held. But, of course, you had to be Tip to know these unobtrusive, ordinary weapons that didn't glisten or shine in the flares, but remained hidden in the fold of a tunic or in a cupped, dirty hand. Security weren't alert to anything or they would have felt the sullen thunderous air, the kind that precedes the great Wet.

No, they were blinded by Amos's defenseless stand, deafened by his slightly apologetic tone and when Egan realized that, he started to feel prickles of real panic alerting his spine. What had Amos planned?

He craned around, looking for clues, but there was nothing to see, except the crowd that surrounded him, quietly listening, and the giant figure anchored by crisscrossing ropes to its funeral pyre. Still his hand went down to his hunting knife and he clicked his fingers at Adri to draw her closer to his side. They'd be ready for whatever it was. They were ready.

'It's always your choice,' I told the children. 'It has to be your choice. Some of you will walk away, go back to the despair and loneliness, the voddy and the dope. It has to be your choice. If I make you do something, I'm no better than the Fatters in Glass. You must take responsibility. It's your life.' No one had ever told them that before.

from *The Lessons of Amos from North Tip,*
Healer and Revolutionary

Lulianne walked silently across the great rooftop of Glass. Security should keep surveillance from here. It was the best view of the world. She could see the crowd down at Casino Market. She could see the lines of Security. It made her feel almost uncomfortably visible although no one bothered to look up, they were focused on what was happening down there. Amos had engineered an amazing distraction. Trust Amos.

She slipped back into the shadows of the roof and walked gingerly across to the sliding panels of the hydro labs. It took all her strength to pull one of the panels out, but once it started to move, it moved noiselessly and smoothly. She peered inside. The room was huge. Dim lights lit the rows between the plants and the whole room glowed green. How could there be so much green in the one place? Was this what Egan left behind at Clan? How could he bear to do that?

Someone would have to be guarding all this. Her arms goose-pimpled and she drew back abruptly, nerves tingling, breath held. Counted to a hundred slowly, not once but twice. The green smell filled her nostrils even up where she was. It was fizzy with life and overwhelmed the Tip stink of acrid ash that seemed to permeate her very pores.

She stayed perched, muscles tight with fear but heard nothing. It was impossible, surely, that they'd just let all this grow without having someone watching it? But how long was she prepared to stay there, waiting? Maybe they patrolled on the hour? Maybe she was between rounds?

It was a long drop to the floor — some of the plants were three metres tall and covered in bright fruit. They weren't cramped, either.

Lulianne pulled up the cable and threaded it through one of the metal catches in the glass panel and let it fall to the ground. It was long enough to be used double but would the glass panel break? Probably not at that metal edge. Well, she'd find out. She swung over and began her slide down , using her feet to slow down. Green surrounded her and the smell was unbelievably good. Birdie had claimed that when you died, you flew forever but Birdie had never been here.

Her stomach contracted and gurgled. Hunger, or yearning, gnawed deep inside. There was nothing to do but grab some of the bright leaves off their stems and stuff them in her mouth. They tasted clean and fresh with a hint of sharpness, reminding her of Egan's herbs. She felt for his amulet, held it tightly with her spare hand. If only he could see all this.

She couldn't stop eating even though a bit of her was almost ill with the greed of it.

Some of the leaves were hot, some sweet, others turned almost straight to water, some needled her tongue and the tender roof of the mouth, making her shudder. All the different tastes made her light-headed. Fear dissolved and was replaced with simple pleasure until her stomach felt stretched and full for once and she burped too loudly for the empty room, the noise scaring her back to reality.

The children were somewhere on this floor or the one below, according to Egan's worker contact. It should have been simple. But it was different being here. The first roof panel led to the first hydro lab. According to the map, to the left of the lab were smaller rooms housing equipment. Yes, that was correct. Then on the other side there were more hydro labs.

Small shrubs grew here, a little like the scrubby plants on the way from Death to Glass, except these were glossy green and laden with fruit. Bitter fruit. Lulianne spat one out.

She thought she should follow this passageway up past seven labs, where it would branch off to the right into a large central recreation and growing area. The corridors were horribly open and exposed. There were no shadows or mounds, just metres of bright, clean surfaces.

It was plain stupid to be wandering around dressed like Tip. She back tracked to the first hydro lab. At the back of it was a small equipment room and hanging up, beyond the glass door, an enticing array of clean white coats.

The door was locked. Of course. There were the swipe cards. It was confusing, there was no indication which way to swipe it, just a dull grey strip down one side. There were no instructions anywhere. Obviously everyone in Glass knew how to use them. It wasn't only frustrating but scary. What happened if she put it in the wrong way? Were the doors alarmed for that? Was there some kind of camera surveillance, watching her now as she stood uncertainly in front of the door, turning the card this way and then that?

Lulianne closed her eyes, flipped the card in the air, picked it up and then inserted the side facing her into the lock slot. Nothing happened. Okay, deep breath and turn the card around. An audible click but the door handle didn't give.

'Conting thing,' she swore under her breath. 'How do you work?' Tears prickled at the back of her eyes. She wanted one of those white coats. Angrily she tore the card out, grabbed the handle prepared to try to wrench off and miraculously the handle turned and the door slid open.

The coat was large and fitted well over her own grey clothes. She could almost feel its whiteness through her skin. There was still the problem of her face and hair. She ripped off the bottom of one of the uniforms and wrapped it around her head. Not perfect but better than nothing.

There were proper bathing facilities in Glass. Not like Water where it was all run-off, scummy and almost as grey as everything else. These were gleaming rooms tiled with mirrors so you could see all the bits of you that you never could see otherwise. Mirrors bounced off reflections of you that got smaller and smaller and smaller. Water ran hot and cold. There was soap that lathered in huge scented bubbles. There were pools of water you got into only after you were completely clean. Or that's what they said. Great pools of steam designed to do nothing except have you lie back in them. It would be good to soak in one of them, scrub all the ash off her face, finally be clean.

But she made do with an open tank of water in the hydro lab. It stung her face, biting into it.

The long corridor was still empty. Everything for *them* was beautiful, that's what they said, rooms lit with the flickering of rainbows glancing off a thousand crystals suspended from the ceiling. Ceilings painted with scenes you felt you could wander into. Walls your hand wanted to caress, they were so darkly soft. A recreation room would have to have some outward sign of inner magnificence. So she walked swiftly past the small, utilitarian doors of storerooms and laboratories and looked for a sign.

There it was — a huge double door, painted metal vines snaking up and framing the coloured glass panes that glowed gold, red and green, casting their jeweled light over the white of the corridors. It took all her nerve to touch the handle, formed like a great bulbous fruit and painted in shades of orange and yellow. The slot lock was hidden behind this but Lulianne knew the drill now, slipped the card in and quickly out again and sure enough, the doors opened.

It was a huge space, almost as full of plants as the hydro labs. They weren't in rows, however, but scattered throughout the vast room, forming groups of soothing colours — here a small bush covered with sweet cream flowers, flanked by tall, bunched leaves from the centre of which emerged softly-petalled, intricately shaped flowers. Lounging chairs and small tables were placed strategically near these so a weary body could drop gracefully into the inviting cushions and stretch a languid hand out to the flowers.

Pools of blue and green tinted water were sunk into the floor and more flowers grew in these in a lush tangle of round leaves. Small fountains sent columns of water into the air, splashing it wastefully on the tiled floor and casting flickering shadows on the pale, clean walls.

It would be good to wash her face again, but she didn't. How could you dirty such clean, clean water?

'Lulu!'

'What?'

'Shh, over here.'

She walked cautiously in the direction of the voice towards the far end of the room.

'Lovie!' The girl was in a huge gold-coloured cage, which completely dwarfed her. The floor of the cage was littered with plump cushions and food bowls. A wire swing was suspended from the cage roof above these.

Lovie pressed against the cage, 'How's Ma?' Lovie asked, reaching her small hand through the bars to touch Lulianne.

'She's better, much better,' Lulianne said, holding the girl's hand. 'How are *you*?'

'I'm okay,' Lovie said. 'They just want me for show, like a pet. They want to play with me. The others are still in the storeroom.'

'Do you know where?' Lulianne asked. 'Could you find it, Lovie?'

'I think so. I tried to remember when they brought me here, in case I could get out. But there are so many passages and the doorways. Can you get me out of here?'

Lulianne looked at the cage door. Another swipe-card job.

'That's what the fat one, the General, used,' Lovie said excitedly, pointing to it. 'Can you imagine anyone being fat, Lulianne? Not air fat, flesh fat. You should see what they eat!'

'I've seen the hydro labs,' Lulianne said. 'I ate so much I thought I was going to be sick — just leaves, but they were so good.' The cage door swung open, Lovie stepped out of the cage and they hugged each other, Lulianne lifting the girl right off her feet.

'They don't eat just leaves, ' Lovie said. 'They eat carni all the time, but not dried like we do. This is fresh and tender. They eat as much as they want. Oh Lulianne, you should see them. They're all so ... clean, so soft. Everything is clean and soft. Feel,' she held out a corner of her skirt for Lulianne to touch.

'Yes it is. Come on, Lovie. How are we going to disguise you?'

'No one is around. Some kind of alarm went off and they all went away. We'll be all right, I think.'

'That would be Amos — he started something to draw Security. It must be big. I hope he knows what he's doing. Which way, Lovie?'

'We turn right,' Lovie said uncertainly. 'They're way up the end on this floor.'

They set off down the corridor, with Lovie counting under her breath.

They were on the far side of Glass, Lulianne realised, away from Casino and the market. She was starting to get a hang of the layout of this storey, she thought. There seemed to be a front corridor and a back corridor linking the middle section which was composed of larger spaces, some of them just ornate archways from the front to the back filled with plants and ponds, while others, like the vast recreation room where Lovie had been held, functioned both as rooms and passageways. Others were hydro labs with more plants packed in, all growing riotously.

Everything was polished and shiny. 'The worker robots keep the place clean,' Lovie whispered, her quiet voice echoing in the vast spaces. 'There are more worker robots than Fatters. They do everything. The Fatters just sit around, eating, talking and playing. They *play*, Lulianne. Not dice games, more stupid than that. They have drinking games. They play chasey, like little kids.'

'How far do you think we have to go?'

'A fair way,' Lovie said. 'Lulianne, don't you think that it's strange?'

'What?'

'Everything in here. The way the worker robots do everything and the Fatters do nothing for themselves? The way they live in all this space when there's enough room for us here, too? How they put poison around Tip but grow all these plants in here?'

'We haven't got time to think about all that now, Lovie, I just want to get out of here.' Lulianne said. The space, beautiful as it was, made her feel vulnerable. She didn't stop to admire any of it, just kept hurrying Lovie forward. Another plant, another pond, so what?

'I keep saying,' Lovie said patiently. 'There aren't many people here.'

'But we haven't even seen any worker robots.'

'They'll be busy in the kitchens,' Lovie said. 'Or maybe the labs. I don't think the cleaners are in yet on this floor. Are you okay, Lulianne?'

'I hate this place.' Lulianne shivered. 'I just hate it.'

'You get used to it,' Lovie said. 'You wouldn't think you'd get used to so much, but you do and when you do, it's kind of good, you know?'

'What's good about it?' Lulianne said in surprise.

'Well,' Lovie said slowly. 'It *is* clean. I like it being clean, Lulianne. I don't mean that I like the Fatters. They're stupid, their games are stupid and some of them are just ... mean. But others are okay. It's like they've just forgotten about Out-

130

side. The really fat one, they call the General? He wanted to mate with me and I was real scared. But later this woman, she was old — the oldest person I've ever seen — she came up to me and said he was just nothing but hot air and not to worry about him, and that if he tried anything I had to tell her and she'd stop him. She's his wife, Lulianne, but she cared about me.'

'It doesn't sound as though he cared about her!'

'I guess not, but don't you think it was good of her?'

'I don't know, Lovie. Why did they round you all up in the first place?'

'She said they just wanted a better life for us, for the children.'

'Do you believe that?'

'No,' Lovie said slowly. 'Not exactly. But I think she did.'

'If you want a better life for someone, you don't round them up in the middle of the night and steal them from their homes.'

'She said they didn't know we had homes. They thought we were all strays.'

'Do you want to go home?' Lulianne strode out, so Lovie had to run to catch up.

'Of course I do. I want to get back to Ma. Slow down, Lulianne!'

'Shh!' Lulianne said, stopping suddenly. 'What's that noise?'

There was a mechanical roar Lulianne couldn't identify.

'It's okay,' Lovie said. 'They're cleaning. It must be later than I thought. We can walk past them. They won't notice us and if they do, they won't care.'

'Don't be silly. I'm not just walking past anyone.'

'I tell you, they're on so much dope, they won't see us,' Lovie said dismissively. 'And anyway, they're not going to do anything.'

'There must be another way.'

'Come on, Lulianne, hurry up.'

'No, Lovie. We can't do that.'

'Just come on, Lulianne.' The girl tugged Lulianne's hand.

Lulianne stared down at her. 'I can't just walk past.' To her annoyance her voice sounded weak and frightened.

'You can. Keep your head up and follow me. Sweep past like you own the city. That's all you have to do. I know. Watch me!'

Lovie strode off down towards the noise, her head held high. There was nothing to do but follow. It's an act, that's all. I have to copy her, just like I copied Birdie. Breathe, breathe, go! Lulianne straightened her shoulders and glided after Lovie, looking straight ahead of her. Her heart was thumping so loudly it seemed to echo through her rib cage. What if they weren't worker robots, but were Security. What if they were both just shot?

But Lovie was right. Two worker robots were busy in the opening, one operating a large machine that seemed to be washing and polishing the spotless floor, the other taking the covers off cushions, stuffing them in a big bag and re-placing them. They didn't even look up as the girls swept past them, just bent lower over their task, like zombies.

'See,' Lovie hissed when they were out of earshot. 'They don't think to see anyone other than the Fatters, so they don't. They're out of it on dope. All the workers are. We could just about live here, keeping low. There are empty rooms everywhere. Glass is too big for the Fatters. Imagine living here. We'd have all we wanted to eat, soft things to wear, and no one would even notice us.'

'I don't want to live here. It's creepy. What's come over you?' Everything was *too* clean. She longed for a bit of mud or dust. She wanted to run dirty fingers along the walls, to mark the shiny surfaces. She wanted her sweat to taint the air. 'It even smells wrong in here,' she said. 'You'd think with all these plants it would smell like the hydro labs. Now they did smell good.'

'They pump a smell through the rooms they use. It's a bit sickly, isn't it?'

'It all makes me sick,' Lulianne answered. 'I just want to get the others and get out.'

'We must be getting closer, see how it's getting grubby?'

'Sort of.'

'They don't come into this part often and I think the worker robots don't bother to clean it. It's a sort of storage area — all sorts of weird things, Lulianne, even in the room they kept us in.'

Compared to Tip this part of Glass was still immaculate. You'd eat your food from the floor, even. It was dirtier, though — there wasn't the same lustre. Lulianne started to relax. This was more her kind of place.

'There were Security,' Lovie whispered. 'But only two. I guess they figured kids couldn't do much. They doped us when they put us in the transport. That knocked me out but I think some of the others were okay. Tick, Ned and Burr faked it. I don't think anything could knock Burr out. She's tough as salt bush. They'll be planning something.'

It was hot, oppressively so, in this part of Glass, and the overhead lights were dimmed down to almost nothing.

'That's it,' Lovie pointed to a double door ahead. 'There was supposed to be Security at the door, too, but when they took me, the others left because it wasn't cooled and they wanted to start a dice game downstairs. They said it didn't matter. We didn't need *proper* guarding. It's a big space beyond that, but not grand. Just like a huge dump for everything they don't want.'

'Okay,' Lulianne looked at the doors with despair. Unlike the other doors in Glass, they were completely solid. These were plain metal doors with no ornamentation whatsoever. 'Where are Security?'

'Playing cards. They'd set themselves up under the light. They change shifts, Lulu, maybe we get in then?'

The two girls stared at the impassive doors.

'There's no cover here,' Lulianne said.

It wasn't strictly true. They were crouched in an alcove area which offered them some concealment but Lulianne hoped Lovie wouldn't think of that. The whole place gave her the heebie-jeebies and even though she could hear Egan's voice in her head counseling patience, she couldn't listen. He wasn't here, in the shadowy gloom, separated from the children by just a door. Well, not just a door, she corrected herself, a heavy pair of blank metal doors staring back at her like blind eyes. 'I wonder if we took them by surprise ...'

'I don't know. It's risky.'

'It might be like the cleaners. How they didn't see us because they didn't think we existed. Suppose we just burst in. It would be the same thing, wouldn't it? They'll think it's more Security or Fatters. They won't think of a rescue party.'

'Have you got any weapons?'

'I've got knives. Can you handle a knife?' She drew the knives from her pouch, flicked one open and handed it to Lovie.

'I can throw anything,' Lovie said proudly. 'Amos taught me how.'

'I'll use a swipe card, the door will open and we'll walk in. We'll have an instant when we catch Security off guard, just because they won't be expecting us. But it will only be an instant. They'll be armed, right?'

'They're always armed,'

'We'll be able to do it. We've got the most important element of any fight on our side — surprise.'

'Okay.' Lovie balanced the knife across her fingers. 'With a knife this good I can hit the target right on, nine times out of ten.'

'Well, let's hope you can do that again.' She found her own knife, and the small pellet of gunpowder that Egan had made up for her. It wouldn't do anything except make a loud noise, but Security didn't know that.

'We can't afford to muck this up, Lovie, we have one chance and that's all. We go in and get them any way we can. If we have to kill them, we kill them. Right?'

'Right.' Lovie held her knife like a professional.

Lulianne swiped the card. Her hands were steady but her heart galloped like a wild pacca. The doors opened. Even Lulianne, used to quickly scanning a crowd, found it difficult to make sense of the long room's chaos. There were pallets and children sleeping, doped or pretending to be doped everywhere and not a Security to be seen. The pallets weren't laid out in orderly rows but were strewn randomly around the room. No one stirred. Lulianne felt the hairs on the back of her neck prickle. Was everyone dead? But when she looked more closely, she could see chests rising and falling, and then she became aware of small sounds, the sighs of people sleeping, a snuffle here and there and some intermittent snoring.

Suddenly they heard their names whispered urgently: 'Lovie, Lulu! Over here.'

'Tick,' Lulianne exclaimed. 'Are you okay?' Beside her, Lovie gasped and ran to her sister.

'Oh, it's good to see you, Lovie,' Tick said. 'I thought you were dead.'

'Is Ned okay?' Lovie asked, clinging to her sister.

'Yeah, he's all right.'

'Where's Security?' Lulianne said. 'We need to work fast, Tick.'

'Security.' Tick snorted with derision and pointed to two pallets practically opposite hers. 'On the dope. Had to do a double shift — orders came through last night. Ha! Were they mad! So they took most of the dope themselves. I'm on shift. We take it in turns to keep watch. We'd have got out by now except that not even Security can get out. How did you get in?'

'Swipe cards.'

'That's worth more than cash. We've tried everything while Security's been out of it. There's no way out without swipe cards. When they finish a shift, Security swipes them in, then they give the shift that's leaving their swipe cards. We're all locked in together.' Tick was up now. 'Come on, let's them tie together. There'll be something we can use.'

'I've got some rope. We'll secure them with that. Quickly, before they wake up. Though there's not enough rope here to do them both. We'll have to tie them together somehow. Can we move them?'

'Here, I'll help,' Ned joined them, giving his sister a quick hug. 'Drag the pallets together. Less chance of them waking if we do that. You go take the foot, Tick. Lovie, Lulianne and I will take the head.'

As they dragged the pallets closer, an empty voddy bottle rolled off.

'No wonder they're out to it,' Ned whispered, 'if they drank all that with the dope they took.'

'Sshh,' Tick hissed, watching one of the men.

The children froze. The man's eyelids flickered and he muttered something before rolling over towards his companion. He didn't wake up.

'How much rope?' Nick mouthed at Lulianne.

Silently she held the piece up.

'That's all?'

Lulianne nodded.

'Can't do much with that. We need more. Lovie, have a scavenge. You too, Tick. We'll guard these fellows.'

More of the children were stirring. Burr came up to Ned and stood close to him. They conferred in whispers and she went away quickly, gathering up the waking children and shepherding them away. The only sound in the room was the snoring of Security and the odd shuffling noise from the scavengers at the back. It was unnaturally quiet as though everyone was breathing more slowly. The children were grouped together near the great doors but there was a watchfulness about them, too, as though they were ready to spring. Packs of dogs looked like that, guarding new litters of pups.

'All we could find,' Tick said in her ear. 'I don't know how strong it is?' She handed Ned a roll of tape. He pulled some out with a loud tearing noise.

'It's sticky one side.' He nervously checked the men who slept on, oblivious. 'It'll have to do. Let's get their hands first, then they won't be able to shoot.'

'Can we get the weapons?'

'Not without a swipe card. They're fixed around them.'

Lulianne pressed a swipe card into his hand.

'You've got everything, a conting miracle, you are, Airdancer!'

'Come on,' Tick said quietly, 'we've got to move.'

The pallets were close enough to rope the two men together, but their hands were all in the wrong position. One man had his jammed between his thighs, the other had one under his cheek and one resting on his hip.

Ned beckoned to Burr who came straight away.

'We need help,' he mouthed and clenched his fist to indicate muscle. Burr nodded and glided away.

The children grouped around Security and Ned counted, using his finger. 'One, two, three,' At the third gesture they pounced on the two men.

'Wharr the conting.'

'Gerroff, you conting louses. Whaddya think ya doin?'

But the men, heavy with dope, were no match for the children who pinned them down and lashed them together at the wrists and ankles, trussing them up quickly and efficiently, ignoring the swearing.

The silence in which they worked was eerie and unnerved their prisoners.

'It's not going to get you anywhere,' one said, 'you can't get out.'

The children didn't reply. Ned yanked the shoulder strap of the automatic around so the electronic locking device was facing out.

'Hey, you can't ... you need ... you haven't ... they'll conting kill me if ...'

Ned swiped the card, the lock clicked and released the strap. He tugged the rest of it free from the man. 'We have weapons,' he grinned. 'We're an army, kids.'

There was a ripple as the children applauded in silence, touching their palms together.

The strangest army, Lulianne thought, surveying their pinched, dirty faces, the scars and sores that decorated them. But they'd worked together better than any unit she'd seen in Defense. They were more disciplined than those frontier mercenaries.

'Okay, we've got to get out of here.'

'We're not getting out,' Ned's tone was surprised. 'We're in here now.'

'No Ned! We've got to get out.'

'This is it ... What Amos has been talking about. This is our chance to change history.'

'This is your chance to get home safe.' Lulianne said, 'back to Tilley. It's not time, Ned. You need more people than this. You need adults. More weapons. A plan. A strategy. More time and planning. We've got, what? Two automatics and two knives against the whole of Glass. Forget it!'

'What will they do when they find us gone and these guys roped up?'

Tick nudged one of the Security men with her foot.

'It doesn't matter, we'll be away by then. We can work that out.'

'It does matter,' Ned said. 'It matters, Lulu. They could just come down on Tip with everything they've got. They could kill us all.'

'They can't. They need us. The Fatters need us,' Lovie said, 'I heard them, all the time. They're scared of dying out. They can't kill us. We're their last hope.'

'I want to fight,' Burr picked up one of the automatics, clicked the strap lock shut and slung it over her shoulder and aimed the barrel at the Security men. 'I want to kill the Fatters. Get rid of them all.'

'What the cont is she doing? C'mon we just do our job.'

'That's what everyone says.'

'Don't waste the ammo,' Ned said, 'we've gotta think this through.'

Burr lowered her weapon. 'You sure I can't just get 'em?'

'It's ammo.'

'Kick 'em then?' Burr aimed her foot towards the genitals of the nearest man, who winced and tensed in response.

'Don't waste it, Burr. I think,' Ned addressed them all, 'I think that the Airdancer could be right. I don't want to do that but it might be right.'

'Amos was doing something outside, he probably has plans.'

'It's started already,' Lovie interrupted. 'They all left, the Fatters, and went to talk about it.'

'Okay, so that means we should be outside. What we should do is to get out quick but with some weapons. Where are they?'

'Wouldn't these wankers know?' Burr dug her toe into one of the men's thighs and prodded. 'Come on, where are the weapons?'

The Security exchanged a glance and shook their heads.

'You don't know, or you won't tell us?'

'Classified.'

'I'd better shoot their kneecaps,' Burr said. 'That'd hurt, Amos told us.'

'C'mon Grun, she's mad enough to do it.'

'You'd better know.' Burr's finger tightened on the trigger. 'I'm crazy, aren't I Ned?'

'You are.'

'We're under orders. We'll be disposed. We can't tell. Have some pity.'

'I'll tell you,' the other man watched Burr warily. 'There's a big space on the second floor, Tip side at Casino end. That's where they'll be. The cameras link into there.'

'Shoot the other one?'

'Ammo, Burr. We've got our information. Okay, let's get these guys away. Where we can hide 'em?'

They used the last of the tape to gag the men and then, with some difficulty, rolled them into a low storage cupboard.

'Do you think there's enough air?' Lulianne hovered. They hadn't been all that bad, for Security and to die in a cramped, airless space was cruel.

'Lulianne, get real will you?' Burr shook her head. 'These are the enemy.'

'They'll be fine,' Ned said. 'Come on. We've got scavenging to do! Where's the swipe, Lulianne?'

The children surged out of the room. Lulianne followed more cautiously. The children had taken over their own rescue and it made her anxious.

141

What counts is what you do when you think everything is lost. That's when you know who you are. Until then, you could be anyone.

Aunty Teece, Clan

'This is a remarkable day,' Amos said to the crowd. 'Do you know why? It's a wonderfully remarkable day because for once Casino is empty — everyone's out here. Tip is here, the traders are here, the worker robots and even Security are here. Look around you. Imagine what a force we'd be if we were united for the common good. Imagine how powerful we'd be. Imagine what we could do. Why, we could turn Tip, this bare, dusty, barren land into a paradise. It wouldn't take much — not if we were all involved and we had the kind of resources we know are just beyond us. I want you to imagine standing here, surrounded by lush, green vegetation. I want you to imagine standing here with your bellies full of good food, food we'd grown in good soil. What stands between that and us?'

'The Fatters!' the crowd yelled back and Amos nodded at them.

'I'm afraid so. People like our friend here can't think about sharing. They take and take and take and now they've taken our children, our hope for the future. I think we need to tell him where to go.'

'Burn him, burn him!' the crowd took up the cry. Egan shivered. Behind the corner of Glass, he could see a faint lightening of the sky. It would soon be morning. Then there was a flash, a bang and flames shot up around the General. It must have been wired, he realized with surprise. The fire

142

took off in the dry fuel and the huge figure itself started to burn slowly. At first the flames flickered around the bottom half of the General, casting strange moving lights on his face and the stick figure he was consuming. Then they caught and flames engulfed them both, ash and embers floating into the crowd.

Security moved forward, alert again, hands on their weapons, voddy bottles put away. They were uncertain, though, and the wild, shouting crowd ignored them. People banged pipes together, the drummers started again with renewed vigour. Egan banged on a pipe someone gave him. Tip had erupted in a earshattering cacophony.

Then there was a tremendous explosion and Casino whooshed into flames. Glass, metal struts, all sorts of debris flew everywhere, hitting Security and Tip without discrimination. People screamed and ran, some Security started firing randomly in to the crowd.

'Protect yourselves,' someone shouted.

'Get them!' someone yelled.

People went down. There was smoke everywhere. Egan could only see an arm's length in front of him. He grabbed Adri by the scruff of her neck and had his knife ready in his other hand. He kept moving towards the stage where he'd last seen Amos. There was cover there. He stepped on people who had been hit. There was no time to stop, no time to look. He just kept moving mechanically. A Security loomed up in front of him out of the smoke and Egan struck out, knocking the man to the ground.

'Sorry,' Egan said. 'Sorry.' And stumbled off.

Someone in front of him called out, 'They got Amos, the bastards.' Egan looked up and through the haze, caught a glimpse of the boy, backlit by flames, crumpling to the ground, holding a hand to his shoulder.

'Amos!' Egan shouted. 'Wait! Someone get him! Save him!' He let go of Adri and started running. Amos couldn't die. He wouldn't let him die. A Security fired at him but Egan dodged and zigzagged. Something was beside him, he glanced down and it was Adri, keeping at his heels.

It felt as though hours had passed before he reached Amos, even though the boy was still lying where he had fallen.

'Amos!' Egan said urgently. 'Amos, it's me.'

'Egan, I'm hit bad,' Amos said. 'Can't talk.'

'Here you, help me. Let's get him under the stage, to shelter.'

Between three of them they carried Amos under the stage where he wouldn't be trampled. Egan stripped some clothes off a Security corpse — they looked clean at least — and tore them into bandages.

'I wish you were doing this to me,' he said. 'You've got the know-how.'

'No, you don't. You need to be alive. For when the Airdancer comes back. You're doing well.'

Egan sat back on his heels. Amos was grey but he was still smiling. He reached for Egan's hand, wincing at the movement.

'I think we've done it,' he said. 'I think we've brought down Glass.'

Egan gripped his hand. 'You might be right,' he said. 'Some distraction, Amos.'

Amos laughed, a short sound that turned into a gargling noise.

144

There was blood everywhere — bloody fingerprints on Egan's hand, blood seeping through the dressing and blood on the ground.

'Stay with us, Amos.' Egan pleaded, 'We need you.'

'I'm not going far,' Amos whispered. 'Just sleeping for a while, that's all. It's a shock, that's all. Stay here? Just while I have a little sleep?'

'Of course,' Egan said. 'I'll be right here when you wake up, Amos.'

He cradled Amos's head in his lap and stroked the young man's face with his fingers. The noise of the crowd and the fires retreated as he concentrated his thoughts on healing Amos. Each of his fingers was a ray of white light. The light was ever-replenishing and all powerful. Each time he touched his friend's face, the light entered Amos. It was all he could do.

Some infections go so deep you have to dig out good flesh just to get rid of the bad. You hate doing it but you need to save the patient so you keep digging, sacrificing the good along with the bad.

from *The Lessons of Amos from North Tip,*
Healer and Revolutionary

'What was that?' Lulianne stopped, panting, as the whole of Glass shook.

'It's Casino,' Ned shouted, at a window. 'Look!'

'We've got to be there.' Burr grabbed his hand, 'come on, we've got to be there. They need us. Forget weapons, let's just go! Lovie, do you know the way?'

Lovie took the lead, and the rest of them swarmed after her. They ran efficiently and quietly, their feet making little noise on the polished floors. Lovie led the way effortlessly back through the room where she'd been held prisoner and on.

'No looting,' Ned wasn't even panting. 'Just go.'

The first deaths were on the central stairs.

'Conting hell,' Burr shouted, 'it's Fatters!' She opened fire and the first three went down, surprised looks on their faces.

'Down,' Ned shouted. 'Burr you conting idiot!'

The kids scattered behind the only protection, the huge carved metal banisters of the staircase.

'Lucky, eh? This is like armour!' Burr laughed as the Fatter's bullets pinged uselessly off the metal. 'This is good!' She ducked around and fired again. 'Got another.'

'Ahh!'

'That was one of ours,' Lulianne started up but Burr grabbed her by her dreads and pulled her back down.

'Drop! Nothing we can do yet.'

It seemed to go on forever, Ned and Burr ducking up and firing, the bullets richocetting wildly around. So this is what death sounds like, Lulianne thought, huddled where she was, listened, cursing her useless knife.

'They're going!' Ned shouted. 'We've scared 'em off.'

Three of the kids were wounded but not badly. The pressed metal had served its purpose.

'They'll be getting Security, Ned. We don't have time to deal with injuries.'

'Everyone can walk, Burr, we're not leaving behind anyone who can walk.'

Lulianne didn't think she could touch the dead Fatters, not even to get the much needed guns. It wasn't so much the blood, though that was bad enough. Burr pushed her to one side, heaved one of the corpses over, grabbed the gun, wiped it on the Fatter's shirt and gave it to Lulianne.

'You do what you have to,' she said. 'I'm crazy, but I'm not killing crazy. I just want to bring my kids up with full bellies and something to live for. Do you understand?'

Lulianne nodded.

'Can you use it?'

'I don't know.'

'We haven't time for a lesson, but aim true and watch the kick back. You'll be fine.' She touched Lulianne lightly on the shoulder.

'The stairs are clear,' Ned called them all to attention. 'We don't have to worry about them.' From where they were standing the stairs spiraled down to the ground level. 'It's the landings on each level we have to watch. We'll go in groups. Don't shoot unless you have to. Each group needs two guns.'

They weren't ambushed until the ground level when Security came from both directions.

'Stop! Or we'll shoot!'

The kids left on the stairs dropped. The ones on the landing stopped — but just for a second. Then Burr and Ned fired in apparent unison.

'Conting hell, they've got weapons!'

'We've got orders!'

'Stuff the orders. Get out of here!'

The Security turned and ran.

'Quick!' Ned yelled. 'Go, go, go!'

The other groups tumbled down the stairs. Ground level!

'Get cover!' Ned shouted just as an explosion blasted Glass, the great doors of the city cracked open and debris rocketed around everywhere.

A quiet whimpering woke Lulianne. She was lying behind a pillar, still miraculously intact.

'Are you allright,' she asked the sound, not daring to move her head.

'I think so,' Tick hiccupped. 'I think I'm okay. Are you?'

Her head throbbed but she could move her fingers and her toes. That was a good sign. Someone had told her that once upon a time. Her head was bleeding, but it wasn't bad. There was a lump. She wriggled around to face Tick.

The girl was covered with grey ash. Tears left clear tracks through it. One of her arms was twisted unnaturally but other than that she looked uninjured.

'I'm scared.'

'So am I.'

They clung together for a minute, breathing in each other's fear.

'How's it going,' Ned crawled up, commando style, heedless of the broken glass that surrounded them. Blood dribbled down his face from a cut above his eye. 'I think part of Glass just blew up. We should get out before the whole place goes up. Can you move?'

'Yeah. What about the others?'

'We've lost a couple. Scrap was hit by something. She's a goner. Can't move. Nat's bad, bleeding. I can't see Jezz anywhere and there are a couple of others. Lovie's fine. She's not even hurt. Burr's got a gash on her arm, but she's okay too. Keep down but move towards the doors. It's conting mayhem out there. You could be killed by anyone.'

The air was thick with stirred-up dust and the smell of blood, glass kept smashing down among them and the shouting and cries of the injured seemed to make Lulianne's head hurt worse.

'That whole wall's going to go,' Ned whispered, grabbing her arm. 'We've got to go. We've got to go back up. Conting hell, watch it!'

Clan isn't just a place. It's what we are, wherever we are. We can leave Clan and still take it with us. It's in our hearts. Wherever you are, you can come back to Clan.

                                        Aunty Teece, Clan

The second explosion woke Amos, or perhaps Egan's fingers nudged him into consciousness.

'Hey, Egan.' He said it so quietly Egan thought at first he was hearing things.

'Amos?'

'Prop me up. What's going on?'

'Glass is exploding,' Egan said. 'Are you sure you can sit up?'

'Yeah. I'll be okay. Oh my god! You're right. Hell! That wasn't supposed to happen. Who calculated those explosives?'

'The kids are still in there.' Egan rubbed the tears out of his eyes. 'Lulianne … it's all gone, all gone.'

'You don't know that,' Amos leaned into his friend. 'You don't know that yet. What do you feel?'

Egan shut his eyes. It was hard to remember Lulianne's face, not all of it at once. He could see pieces of it — how her dreads fell over her temples and how she pushed them behind her ears. He could see the colour of her eyes. He could almost feel her skin under his fingers but he couldn't see all her face at once. Was she dead or alive?

He remembered the amulet. The river rock was smooth on one side and carved with a speed blessing on the other. There were metal, seed and wooden beads on either side and the string was intricately knotted with protective spells.

'She's alive,' he said finally. 'The string is unbroken.'

'What did I tell you? Out of these ashes, we'll coax a new city, a city for us all, Egan. A beautiful place. Look around, what do you see?'

'People dying.'

'Look again, friend. Tell me everything, Egan. Be my eyes.'

Egan peered through the haze. People were dying. But people were also helping the living. Voddy bottles were being passed around, but nobody was drinking. They were using the alcohol to swab wounds. A Security tore bandages from the uniforms of his colleagues and passed them to a Tipper who was bandaging the injured.

'I've got to go,' Egan told Amos. 'You're right. Lulianne will be in there and there'll be stuff to scavenge. I know some of what we need. Seeds, plants, medicine, stuff maybe others will overlook. I'll leave Adri with you. You'll be okay?'

'Don't journey too far, little brother.'

He wasn't just looking for seeds and plants. He was looking for Lulianne.

Amos was right, there was hope. There had to be. He reached the entrance of the city just as that whole section of Glass imploded.

In the end a war is won with more than bombs or guns. It's won by spirit. Tip had spirit. Hell, it was practically all we did have.

from *The Lessons of Amos from North Tip, Healer and Revolutionary*

'Get out of here, now.' Ned yelled. 'Everyone. Move!'

Lulianne knew she was running. She held one hand to her head, she was scared it would explode like Glass if she didn't. Tick grabbed her hand and they dragged each other along. They couldn't look behind them. Glass shards flew everywhere, cutting their feet. Ned and Burr were ahead, running side by side. Then a flying lump of metal whacked the girl and Burr fell to the ground, yanking Ned down with her.

'Run!' Lulianne screamed. 'Ned, run!'

The wall was collapsing behind them. Ned was bent over Burr. Her head was mashed on one side. She wasn't breathing.

'Run!' Lulianne ordered him. 'Go, Ned. Look — it's starting to burn. We've got to go up.'

'Burr's dead. I can't leave her.'

'You have to, Ned, you have to come with us. We have to get out. The whole place could go up in flames. You don't want to be burnt to death.'

'I can't leave her.'

'She's gone. She's gone already. Come on.' She pulled him up.

When they got to the second level they stopped. It was impossible to see anything for the smoke.

'Cover your faces,' Lulianne shouted, 'and keep going up.'

'We're going to die in here,' one of the kids panted. 'After everything.'

'We're going to the hydro labs, there's water there. Come on.'

The hot air blasted up and the noise of the fires was incredible. They passed people as they pushed on, Security and Fatters, going every which way, half veiled and as desperate as the children.

It was cooler on level four and there was less smoke. They straggled back to the hydro labs where they all sank onto the cool tiled floor and lay panting and coughing.

Ned was weeping. Lulianne did a head count.

'We've lost seven.'

'What do we do now?'

'We go through the roof,' Lulianne said. 'It's the only way, Lovie. We're all airdancers now!'

'How do we do that?'

The pouch was still around her neck. She slipped it off, careful not to take off Egan's charm too, and pulled out the cable. 'We climb down this.'

'No!'

'It's the only way. You'll need something to protect your hands with. Plastic, cloth, anything will be better than nothing.'

She went through to the store room where she'd stashed her pack. Seeing the gloves again was like seeing old friends. Egan had tied these on to her when? Yesterday? Was he still alive? She held the stone amulet, *please be alive, Egan. Please be waiting for me.*

Out in the labs the kids were eating plants while they scavenged. They found rope and tape, tore up old uniforms and bound each other's hands and injuries. Ned was the only one who didn't move but they brought him things to eat, fed him as though he was a baby and Tick lifted first one and then the other of his hands up for Lovie to bind with a thick tape she'd found.

The food put new life temporarily into the kids but they were on their last reserves of strength.

'Okay, you there, what's your name?' Lulianne was in charge again. Flying was her territory.

'Skate.'

'Okay, Skate, you're pretty tall. You stand here and we'll leg everyone else up on to the roof.'

'What about us? What do we do after they're all up there?'

'They'll take the cable up with them then they'll drop it down for us, got it? Here, I'll tape your hands first, and then you do mine.'

Even bits of the roof were hot by the time Lulianne and Skate got up there. The kids looked like children again, not like an army. They were standing around, pale and shaking from exhaustion. Ned was slumped down, holding his arm.

'Okay,' Lulianne said gently, 'this is the last bit. We'll go down the cable one by one and wait for each other at the bottom, right? We've all done this before in Circus class.' No one said anything. They were simply too tired.

'Be careful of the walls. You need to swing out from them in case any of them explode with the heat. We're on the far side, though, so it shouldn't be too bad. Anchor the rope when you hit the ground and drag it as far from Glass as you can. Here, you — what's your name?'

'Din.'

'Okay, Din, you look the heaviest. You go first. Hold the

154

rope as best you can. Lovie'll come down next. She's pretty light and then Tick. You should be okay then, to hold it pretty steady for everyone else.'

It was slow. The kids went over obediently, some so slack-muscled they looked as though they'd just fall off the cable but they didn't. Even those who were shaking with fear and exhaustion held on to the end.

Finally Lulianne and Ned were the only ones left. The cable had held up. It was fine. A group of children anchored it at the bottom.

'Come on, General Ned,' she shook him gently. 'It's time to go.'

'Don't want to. Not without Burr. I loved her, Lulianne.'

'I know, I worked that out, Ned.'

'I can't go on.'

'We need you, Ned. You're our leader. What would we have done with you? You can't give up now. We can't re-build Tip without you.'

'It's burning.'

Just as he said that there was a roar and they both looked down from the roof, expecting to see another fire or explosion. The noise didn't come from the ground, however, it came from the sky. They lifted their faces.

'What?'

'Oh, it's rain.' Lulianne stuck her tongue out to catch the heavy drops. 'Come on Ned. It's rain. The Wet's come.'

He started to laugh. She didn't know why but she laughed with him.

'Bloody Burr,' he said, coughing. 'She sent this, you know that, don't you?'

'She loved you.' She had to get him down the cable before it got dangerously slick with water. 'Come on Ned.'

She watched him reach the bottom. The rain pelted down steadily. She stroked the carved side of the amulet with her thumb. Egan would be waiting at the bottom with Adri. She grasped the cable and swung out. The tape on her hands tore a little and she could feel the cold, wet cable against her palm. She lost control close to the bottom and landed awkwardly, twisting her ankle. The ground held her like the softest bed and the rain was Gran's shower. Then she was lifted into the air and a great cheer went up.

'Hip, hip, hooray for the Airdancer of Glass. Hip, hip,' 'hooray!'

They hoisted her up and carried her right around to the front of Glass.

'Three cheers for the Airdancer!' Everyone was shouting it. New people held her up, the children dropped away. She didn't know who was holding her up. Some of them looked like Security.

'Lulu! Lulu!'

'Egan! Let me down. I have to get down now!' But the crowd holding her marched inexorably on. 'Egan,' Lulianne shouted, 'are you okay?'

'Yeah, and so's Amos. Wait for me,' he yelled, and began to run after them, catching up and taking his place in the crowd. 'I love you,' he said. The crowd around them whistled and whooped.

'The Airdancer and the Gardener of Glass!' someone yelled and the rest of them took up the cry.

'We can't go to Clan,' Egan said when the noise died down a little. 'We have to build Clan here, Lulu. We can do it!'

'Let me down,' Lulianne said. 'Please let me down.'

'Let the lass down,' a woman said. 'She needs to hold her man.'

They lowered her to the ground and Lulianne, blushing but resolute, stepped toward Egan. Blessed by the clean rain, they stood and held each other until the crowd slowly dispersed, going back to their business of tending to the wounded, counting the dead, salvaging a new beginning from the rubble of the past.

Glass smouldered, the interior lit by the occasional flare of fire from its depths. People milled around. A group of people wearing Tip clothes too small for them huddled together weeping — badly disguised Fatters. Who cared? It was the end of Glass for them all, Fatters and Tippers alike.

'It's a chance to get it right this time,' a voice startled her from Egan's embrace. 'What do you think, friends?'

'Amos! Thank the heavens you're alive!' Lulianne hugged the thin boy, careful to avoid the stained bandage which bound his left arm and shoulder.

'Well done, Airdancer. I knew you could do it.'

'Not without Egan, or you or the kids. We all did it.'

'We did it together and now the real work starts.' Amos looked over the ruins. His face was so pale, his eyes looked like dark stones. He smiled, anyway. 'Children with full bellies,' he said. 'Something to work for, I reckon.'

'And clean water.' Lulianne tipped her head back and let the rain trickle into her open mouth.

'Plants,' Egan said dreamily. 'Any seeds we can find, this rain'll start them off. We can start planting as soon as you like, Amos. We'll grow ourselves a new city!'

They didn't know what many of the seeds were but they
planted them anyway. Some grew into spiky bushes with
strange flowers, the petals of which were like feathers. We
called them feather trees. My father had a name for each
one. He'd walk there in the evenings and recite the names to
me. My favourite bush, the one I told my secrets to was
Burr. She was my Name Aunty even though I never knew
her. She died in the Revolution but she still lives with us be-
cause we tell her story.

Burr, Glass Clan